Eager For You
(EagerBoyz 1)

H.L Day

Other books by H.L Day

Too Far series
A Dance too Far (Too Far #1)
A Step too Far (Too Far #2)
Temporary Series
A Temporary Situation (Temporary; Tristan and Dom #1)
A Christmas Situation (Temporary; Tristan and Dom #1.5)
Temporary Insanity (Temporary; Paul and Indy #1)
Fight for Survival series
Refuge (Fight for Survival #1)
Standalones
Time for a Change
Kept in the Dark
Taking Love's Lead
Edge of Living
Christmas Riches
Short story
The Second Act

Copyright

Cover Art by H.L Day
Edited by Alyson Roy - Royal Editing Services
Proofreading by Judy Zweifel at Judy's Proofreading
http://www.judysproofreading.com[1]

Eager For You © 2019 H.L Day

All Rights Reserved:

This literary work may not be reproduced or transmitted in any form or by any means including electronic or photographic reproduction, in whole or in part, without express written permission.

Eager For You is a work of fiction. Names, characters, places, and incidents either are the product of the author's imagination or are used fictitiously, and any resemblance to actual persons, living or dead, business establishments, events, or locales is entirely coincidental.

Warning

Intended for an 18+ audience. This book contains material that may be offensive to some and is intended for a mature,

---

1. http://www.judysproofreading.com/

adult audience. It contains graphic language, explicit sexual content, and adult situations.

THANKS

Huge thanks to my beta readers Barbara, Sherry, Fiona, and Jill.

Chapter One

ANGEL THREW HIS HEAD back and let out a long-drawn-out moan, his fingers making indentations in the ass he'd been pounding for the last hour as he pulled out. It only took a couple of strokes after ripping the condom off to paint the guy's muscular ass cheeks. He breathed heavily, taking a moment to admire the way his cum stood out starkly against the tanned skin. He dipped a finger into one of the larger puddles, smearing it downward over one of the taut globes, the muscle contracting under his touch.

A desperate plea ended any further attempts he might have made at cum art. "Need to come, Angel. Need it real bad. Wanna come all over your chest."

Angel levered himself off his partner and flipped onto his back, his head resting against the pillows. The guy wasted no time in straddling him, his muscular thighs squeezing Angel's hips tightly. As his partner wrapped his hand around his cock and began to stroke it, Angel played his part to perfection, painting a look of lust on his face as he ran his hands over the guy's body, pausing every now and again to tweak a nipple or to palm his balls. "Yeah, Cain, come for me. I want to see how much cum that big cock of yours produces." The thighs gripped him tighter, the hand moving faster until it was almost a blur. They moaned in unison as Cain went still, his muscles tensing with a look of ecstasy on his face. Then there was the hot splash of cum on Angel's chest as Cain's cock spurted several times, the cum settling in the rivulets of Angel's defined six-pack. Just like Angel had, Cain dipped a finger, coating it with the viscous fluid before bringing it to Angel's lips with a smile on his face. Angel opened up obediently, sucking the digit inside and swirling his tongue around it to taste.

"Cut."

Angel pulled the face he hadn't been able to pull with the camera still running. Tasting cum was never his favorite part of the job. It always proved popular with the viewers, though. His fault probably for making them believe he loved it when he'd first started out. Now if they went a few scenes without him tasting any cum, they made a fuss, speculating about what it could mean. *Has Angel got a jealous boyfriend? One that's told him he can't taste anyone else's cum? Has he got some sort of secret problem with his scene partner? What's he done? What's his partner been eating to make his cum taste bad?* Angel had heard it all. Over and over again.

When Cain seemed in no hurry to climb off him, he tapped his thigh. Thankfully taking the hint, Cain swung his leg back over, maneuvering himself over to the side of the generously sized bed before clambering to his feet and coming to stand next to it just as Evan, the director and studio owner, strolled over to them. "Good job, boys. We got plenty of footage. Lots of passion. Viewers are going to love this one." He winked at Angel. "Not that they don't love everything you do. I reckon we could have you reading the phone book and they'd eat it up."

Angel laughed. "Not unless I had my dick in my hand at the same time. Although, I think even I'd struggle to jerk off to the phone book. You'd have to stick some interesting pictures in there to make it work." Evan's glance dropped to Angel's abdomen, the trickle of cum starting to make its way onto the sheets. His gaze moved across to Cain. "I've never seen you come that much before. You've drenched our poor boy here."

Cain looked mighty pleased with himself. "Well, I guess someone was hitting my prostate just right." He paused, his smile growing wider. "I'd definitely be up for a repeat performance sometime."

Evan shrugged. "We'll see. Schedule is pretty full for the next few months. Unfortunately, Angel insists on sleeping, and despite what you might have heard about him, his dick's not good to go several times in one day." He twisted around and picked a towel up off the back of a chair, offering it to Angel.

Glad of a chance to get rid of the rapidly drying cum on his abs, Angel eagerly accepted it, wiping at his abdomen as he addressed Evan. "Do you need any shower footage?" He didn't miss the hopeful look on Cain's face. Someone seemed to have developed a bit of a crush on him in the last few hours while they'd been filming. It happened sometimes, particularly with the newbies, who hadn't quite gotten the knack of separating the difference between professional and personal yet. Cain would learn. Either that or he'd get to film with one of the models who didn't give a damn about keeping things separate. Which, from what Angel had heard, was most of them.

Evan shook his head, his shaggy blond hair flying around wildly with the gesture. To Angel, he always looked like he should have been a rock star rather than a porn studio owner and director. "Not this time."

Obviously struggling to hide his disappointment, Cain gave a tight nod before ambling off in the direction of the showers. Angel decided he'd give him ten minutes before following. Hopefully, by that time, he'd have finished and there'd be no chance of any awkward conversations where Angel would be forced to bluntly reject him. That was worth having to sit there a bit longer, smelling of cum that wasn't even his own. He gave Evan an accusing look, wondering if that's why the wily bastard had paired them up in the first place. "You could have warned me."

He gave an evil grin. "What? That someone was carrying a bit of a torch for you?"

Angel rolled his eyes and nodded.

His boss's smile grew even wider. "Sweetheart, they've all got a thing for you. Only difference is that some of them get over it once they've had sex with you, whereas, for the rest, getting up close and personal with you only makes it worse. I guess our lovely Cain there falls into the latter category. I wouldn't worry about it. It wears off. He's got a scene with Blaze next week. Once he's had that monster dick up his ass, he won't even remember your name, never mind your cock."

Laughing, Angel climbed off the bed. There was only the two of them, the cameraman having departed at the same time Cain had. He glanced down at his own dick, now completely flaccid. "Thanks, Evan. Way to make a man feel inadequate."

Evan threw another towel at him. "Stop fishing for compliments. You know your cock's big and you know exactly how to use it. Blaze's dick, however, is huge. He's still not getting anywhere near as many clicks on the site as you are, so you don't have to worry." He jerked his head toward the door. "Now hit the showers. You've probably left it long enough that Cain's not lying in wait and hoping for round two off-camera. You know, it wouldn't kill you to be a bit less stubborn and give yourself a chance for a bit of fun. Cain's a hot guy. You could do a lot worse."

"And you'd be fine with that, would you?" It was a genuine question. Angel had never looked into it so he wasn't entirely clear on Evan's rules or whether there were any.

"I'll tell you what I tell all the boys. On camera first and then you can do whatever the hell you like in your own time."

Angel would be lying if he said he hadn't considered it. The studio was a virtual smorgasbord of hot and horny gay men who all loved sex. But for some reason it just didn't appeal. How were you supposed to know whether they were acting or whether it was real? It was probably pretty hypocritical of him when most of the guys he'd dated were under the impression that he was just a computer sciences student and didn't have a clue what he did on the side. And he meant to keep it that way. Problem was that between his degree and the work at the studio, which paid his bills, it left very little time to meet someone.

He left Evan and headed for the shower, relieved to see that Cain had already gone. It sounded big-headed but it wouldn't be the first time a scene partner had hung around to invite him out for a drink, or been even more straightforward and asked him back to their place to fuck. There was nothing wrong with it. Of course there wasn't. They were all red-blooded males. But it just wasn't his thing. Besides, they'd have certain expectations of him, given his porn persona, that didn't quite align with his personal life. To him, enjoyable as sex for the studio was, it was work and he was happy to keep it that way.

He spent a long time under the hot spray, running through the list of things he needed to get done during the rest of the day. Boring things, mostly university stuff that he needed to make a dent in.

After wrapping a towel around his waist, Angel padded over to get his things out of the lockers where they kept everything while they were filming. Evan liked to start with underwear only so it was essential to have somewhere to stash your clothes. He sat down on one of the benches, pulling his phone out and wincing at the message on the screen.

Mum: *I can't wait to finally meet your boyfriend. He's still coming this weekend, right? I'm was gutted he had to cancel last time.*

Shit! He'd forgotten all about that. Well, maybe forgotten wasn't quite the right word, more pushed it out of his head in the hope that it would go away. Only now, he only had a couple of days before the weekend. And no boyfriend. God knows what had possessed him to claim he was seeing someone. Actually, he did know. It was a couple of things. His mum's insistence on talking about his brother's and sister's significant others, all of who'd been together for at least a year, was one of them. A fact that made him feel like a lame loser.

But the clincher had been his mum reading an article about university costs and pondering aloud exactly how he was managing to pay for everything. In an effort to steer her away from a conversation skating far too close to him having to confess to his secret porn career, he'd made up a mythical boyfriend instead, waxing lyrical about how wonderful he was and how committed to each other they were. The plan had been to leave it a few weeks and then casually drop a break-up into conversation, but she'd been so happy for him that he just hadn't had the heart to do that.

So now he had the problem of her expecting to meet someone who didn't exist. He chewed on his lip as he considered the dilemma. The obvious solution was to come clean, but then she'd start worrying about why he'd made it up in the first place and it would turn into a huge thing which would really put a dampener on her birthday celebrations.

"Hey, are you alright?"

Angel lifted his head to meet the concerned expression of the guy he hadn't even heard come into the locker room. Another one of the newbies. In fact, the newest of the newbies. He'd only been filming with the studio for a few weeks, and up until that point, their paths had never crossed. Not that Angel's path crossed with many of the other models unless he had his cock in them. He liked to get in—to the studio that was, not their ass—get the job done and then get out. He knew some of them socialized after hours, but he'd never joined them, preferring the company of his university mates instead. It kept life simple and that was the way he liked it.

He cast around for the new guy's name. Lane. No, not Lane. It definitely began with an L. Luke? Liam? Leo—that was it. Leo Stone. Same first name as Angel's star sign. He should have remembered it for that reason. Most of the models went by two names except for him. He couldn't even remember why that was, whether it was just that he'd been too lazy to think up a fake surname or whether Evan had done it deliberately to try and create an air of mystery around him. Whatever it was, it had stuck and he'd always gone by just Angel.

Now that he remembered his name, he gave Leo a quick once-over. Shorter than Angel's five-eleven by a good couple of inches. No less muscular though. Never let it be said that Evan didn't have a type when it came to recruiting. Dark cropped hair, stubble, and large brown eyes finished the picture. Going by the bag slung over his shoulder and his casual attire of jeans and a T-shirt, he was just on his way in to film a scene. Angel finally answered the question Leo had asked. "I'm fine."

Leo crossed the floor to stand in front of him. "You don't look fine. Maybe it's something I can help with."

Angel smiled, not entirely sure whether the guy thinking he could help was sweet or irritating. "I doubt it. Not unless you've got a spare boyfriend hanging around that I can borrow for the weekend." What was he doing? Why was he telling a complete stranger this? What had gotten into him?

"You don't have one?"

The chocolate-brown gaze was strangely intent as he took a seat next to Angel on the bench.

He'd started now, so he may as well continue, strange as it was to confide in someone he didn't know. "If I did, then producing one to take home to meet my parents wouldn't be such an issue." Angel chuckled drily as Leo's face creased in confusion. "Don't worry. It's a long story which involves me being a complete idiot and saying stuff that I really shouldn't have said that's now come back to bite me in the ass. The moral of the story is don't tell lies." He rubbed his face. "I guess I'm just going to have to confess." The amount of ribbing he was going to get from his siblings was going to be torturous.

"Why not just get someone to play the part for the weekend?"

The words took him by surprise. It was an interesting idea, but today was Wednesday and he needed to travel there on Saturday. "Right? Like I'm going to find someone willing to travel to Blackpool with me for the weekend and play boyfriend."

"I would." Angel found it hard to say which one out of the two of them seemed more shocked by the words that came out of Leo's mouth. A flush spread slowly from Leo's neck until it reached his face. That was interesting. A porn star who blushed. If he did it on camera, the subscribers would go wild for it. He'd have to mention it to Evan.

Leo coughed. "I mean... I like Blackpool. I haven't been for years and I'm not doing anything this weekend." He lifted one shoulder in a casual shrug. "Coastal air is good for you, right? The offer's there if you want it?"

Angel stared at him, the cogs starting to turn in his brain. Could they pull it off? He'd purposefully kept things vague while talking to his mum, keeping as many details out of it as he could. So Leo not meeting a physical description wasn't going to be a problem. It could work? It was crazy though. It would be far more sensible just to fess up and take the flak that came along with it, or make up some sort of story that they'd had a big argument just before the weekend. He opened his mouth with the intention of telling Leo exactly that. "Are you sure?"

A huge grin lit up Leo's face, his cheeks still flushed. "It'll be fun."

Angel wasn't too sure about that.

Chapter Two

MOONLIGHTING AS LEO Stone had never been part of a deliberate plan for Damian. It had just sort of crept up on him, triggered by a friend of his gloating over how much money he'd made for filming a solo scene. Or as he'd put it, free money for doing on camera what he'd have spent the afternoon doing anyway. Given the friend, it hadn't been a joke—more a statement of fact. As a struggling student, it had seemed like too good an opportunity for Damian to resist. There were two studios Damian knew of who filmed in London. The one his friend had gone to, and one other. The sensible thing would have been to stick to the same one. After all, he had a personal guarantee of everything being above board. Going elsewhere meant there was a risk of walking into a less reputable operation. One he wouldn't know anything about.

Only, *EagerBoyz*—the other studio—had Angel on their books. Angel, the muscled hunk who'd been Damian's default choice for an appointment with his hand for years. He'd watched all his scenes—several times over. Every single one was guaranteed to get him off in record time. There was something about his performances which ticked every box Damian had, from Angel's big cock to the fact that he knew exactly how to use it. Although, it wasn't just the body. He had a smile which seemed to hide a multitude of secrets behind it as if he'd only reveal so much of himself to the viewers behind the camera. It was that air of mystery, along with the face and body, that made him by far the most popular performer at *EagerBoyz*. The subscribers—and Damian—couldn't get enough of him.

Therefore, once Damian had made the decision to go ahead and apply to do a solo, it had been a no-brainer which studio he'd apply for. The solo had led to the offer of more work. A decision he'd agonized over for more than a week before agreeing to go ahead and give it a try. The second scene was a blow job, giving and receiving. He'd known what the next offer would be. The studio liked to follow a familiar pattern: solo, blow job, fuck, with the money offered going up in incremental amounts each time. In the end, he'd taken the leap and gone for it. He liked sex. Why not get paid for it?

It had proved a lot easier than he'd expected. Evan, the studio boss, was a great mixture of professional and considerate. He seemed to know just the right way to put his performers at ease and get a great performance out of them. Damian had forced himself to watch his own scene, surprised by how relaxed he'd come across on camera when he'd been a churning mass of nerves on the inside. It had helped that he'd been put with one of the most experienced performers the studio had.

Not Angel, though.

Their paths had barely crossed in the few weeks that Damian had been filming scenes. He hadn't expected to become best buddies with Angel, but he'd hoped to catch more than a fleeting glimpse of Angel's back as he left the studio. The guy seemed to turn up a few minutes before his scene started and leave a few minutes after. That, and the fact that he never seemed to socialize with the others, meant Damian still saw more of Angel onscreen in the privacy of his own home than he did in real life working for the same company.

Feeling brave, he'd stayed behind one day and had a quiet word with Evan, his heart thumping with a mixture of anticipation and nerves as he'd requested a scene with Angel. Evan had looked thoughtful and told him that he'd pass on the request to Angel and see what he thought of the idea.

Two days later, Evan had pulled him aside and delivered the crushing news. Angel had said no. No reason. No excuse. Just a flat-out refusal. Damian had felt like shit for days. What was wrong with him? Everyone in the studio who stuck around for more than a few months seemed to get paired up with everyone else eventually. Did that mean Angel would eventually change his mind? Or did he have a list of people that were definite no-no's? No matter how long Damian had mulled it over, he hadn't come any closer to coming up with a definitive answer.

Then yesterday, fate had finally seen fit to smile on him, delivering a half-naked Angel directly into his path. It had taken all the willpower he possessed to act cool, rather than drool all over him. And then the perfect opportunity had presented itself. Angel needed a fake boyfriend for the weekend, and Damian was more than happy to step into those shoes. The opportunity had seemed like a gift sent from heaven. A chance for them to get to know each other.

So now, here he was—waiting outside the library where they'd agreed to meet. The plan was for Angel to pick him up in his car and drive the two of them to Blackpool. It gave Damian the space of a weekend to make Angel see him properly. Not as Leo, someone who just happened to work in the same place as

Angel did, but as Damian. Maybe the two of them would hit it off and then who knew what it might lead to? If he was honest, it wasn't just lust he felt for Angel. He'd always harbored the hope that should they ever meet, something would click between them and Angel might reciprocate his feelings.

It was probably a crazy notion which was going to leave him feeling shitty by Monday when it crashed and burned. But he hadn't been able to stop himself from offering his services as a fake boyfriend. There was never going to be another opportunity to get close to Angel and discover who the man behind the persona was.

Except, Angel was late and Damian was beginning to wonder if he'd changed his mind. They hadn't swapped numbers. Therefore, he had no other option but to keep waiting. He hefted his bag more firmly onto his shoulder, taking the opportunity to wipe his sweaty palms on his jeans. *How long should he wait?* He'd already waited ten minutes. *Another ten? Fifteen? An hour? His whole life?*

He was still contemplating the answer to that question when a car pulled up at the curb—a red Toyota, nothing too flashy. The man behind the wheel got out and came around the car to lean against the passenger door. Damian hurried over to him, unable to keep the huge smile off his face. He tried his best to keep his gaze from roving all over the body clad in tight form-fitting jeans and a sleeveless T-shirt which left his muscular arms bare. He managed to restrict himself to a quick once-over without letting it linger. It was the best he could do. "Hey."

Angel wasn't smiling. If anything, he appeared deadly serious. "I wasn't sure if you'd turn up or not. Are we actually going to do this?"

The smile dropped off Damian's face. "You've changed your mind?"

Angel grimaced. "We're never going to be able to pull it off."

Damian stepped closer to him. There was no way now that they'd come this far that he was going to let Angel drive off on his own. One weekend, that's all he needed. Just a chance to satisfy his curiosity and find out whether the man he'd been lusting after for years was simply a pretty face and body, or more than that. He might even discover that the man behind the performance was an absolute douchebag and not worth his time. At least then he might be able to let go of the fascination he carried for the man stood in front of him. He knew deep down that it was a little bit ridiculous to be so gaga over someone he didn't even know, but that didn't mean he'd been able to talk himself out of it.

Maybe a little white lie was in order. Just a little push to shove Angel in the right direction. "You know I'm a drama student?" He wasn't. He was a music student. But they were similar, right? They were both the arts. "So the acting's not going to be a problem for me." That bit was true. Playing the part of Angel's enthusiastic boyfriend would come as naturally as breathing. The difficult part was going to be not letting on that it wasn't an act.

Angel crossed his arms over his chest. "*You* might be good at acting. I'm not."

"You act on camera all the time." Angel didn't offer any response and Damian was forced to stand still while he was subjected to an intense scrutiny that started at the top of his head and worked its way slowly downward until it reached his feet.

If Angel announced that his parents wouldn't buy it because Damian wasn't his type, then he was probably going to spend the rest of the day, if not the entire weekend, huddled underneath his duvet, crying. He steeled himself for rejection, but Angel simply shrugged. "I guess you're right, and you're here now." A muscle ticked in his cheek. "Okay, Leo. Let's do it."

"Damian." His statement was met with confusion, forcing him to elaborate. "If I'm going to be playing the role of your boyfriend, I figure you should probably call me by my real name. Which is Damian. I'm guessing your parents are going to find it a bit strange if I call you Angel all weekend, so you should probably tell me yours as well."

The expression on Angel's face said he was reluctant to release such a juicy piece of information. Obsessed fan that Damian was, he'd looked for the information online but drawn a blank. Angel obviously guarded his privacy fiercely. "I won't tell anyone."

Angel's smile was wry, as if he recognized how ridiculous he was being. He gave a laugh, shaking his head at the same time. "I guess you're going to find out anyway when my parents use it. It's... Josh." He inclined his head toward the car. "We better get going, then. We've got almost a five-hour drive ahead of us and I told my parents we'd be there by mid-afternoon."

Damian was still rolling the name Josh around on his tongue as he stashed his bag in the back of the car before climbing into the passenger seat and fastening his seatbelt. *It's just a name, dude. Calm down.* He'd just about quashed the urge to smile like an idiot by the time Angel had pulled away into traffic. *No, not Angel, Josh.* It was going to take some adjusting to think of him as Josh. He kept repeating the name in his head, hoping it would take root and override the desire to think of him as Angel.

He took the opportunity to study his fake boyfriend while Josh's eyes were focused on the road in front of him. It was weird to be so close to him. He found himself transfixed by his hands on the steering wheel. Hands he'd watched a million times. Stroking his cock. Stroking someone else's cock. Leaving fingermarks on his partners' asses as he'd fucked them. He'd dreamed about those fingers. On him. In him. Touching him. Would he get that chance this weekend? He'd have to, even if it was just as part of the act, right? The thought made him shift in his seat and cover his crotch with his hands, just in case Josh happened to glance over and wondered why he happened to be sporting the best part of an erection.

"Do you mind if I put the radio on, Leo?"

Damian's head snapped up to find Josh staring straight at him, the car stopped at a red light. He must have seen him staring at his hands like some sort of hand fetishist weirdo. He really needed to pull himself together, or Josh was going to be stopping the car and pushing him out in the middle of the road. "Damian."

Josh banged his hand on the steering wheel. "Shit! Right. Sorry. I'm not very good at this am I? I guess subterfuge is not really my thing. So, radio?"

"Don't you think we should talk? I know absolutely nothing about you." *Apart from everything you've said in your videos, which I've committed to memory.* The problem was, that could be absolute bullshit designed to titillate the viewers. Besides, favorite sexual position and the fact that Josh said he had sensitive nipples probably wasn't going to cut it with his parents. It would be nice to get through the entire weekend without being thrown out of their house. "Your parents are hardly going to be convinced we're a couple if we don't know the first thing about each other." Damian was suddenly thrown back in his seat by a sudden swerve to the right as Josh made a last-minute turn. "Or you could just kill me instead. That works as well. Guess then you can tell them that your boyfriend didn't survive the journey."

Josh laughed. A warm glow lit up Damian's chest. He'd made his fake boyfriend laugh. He thought he was funny. This was going to be the best weekend ever. The car slowed as Josh pulled into a service station car park. "I hadn't really thought this thing through properly. I guess I imagined we could just walk in there and my parents would believe me. But you're right. We're not going to last five minutes if we don't get to know each other. I'm not going to be able to concentrate if we do it while I'm driving, so I figured we could stop for breakfast and at least go over the basics. Then we can perhaps add more stuff on the rest of the journey. That way I might at least be able to get your name right."

"We should probably kiss as well." Damian could have kicked himself as soon as the words had left his mouth without having gone anywhere near his brain. He dug his fingers into the edge of the seat—hard—hoping the pain would stop the embarrassment from showing on his face. Only, he could already feel the telltale heat traveling up from his neck.

"What?"

"I just meant..." What had he meant, apart from that he wanted an excuse to kiss him? He couldn't tell Josh that, though. Not without giving away that he was slightly more into

Josh than he'd let on. "We're going to have to be comfortable with each other in order to be convincing."

Josh crooked an eyebrow. "We both make porn. I don't think pretending to be attracted to each other is going to be a problem."

Pretending? Right. Damian schooled his face, this time to hide his disappointment. Only one of them was going to be pretending and it wasn't going to be him. "You mean, you're not always into your scene partners? You..." *Don't tell him that you've watched every scene he's done. Play it cool.* Josh was watching him, waiting for him to finish making his point. He undid his seatbelt, using it as an excuse to look away. "Never mind. Not sure what I was going to say. I need coffee." Besides, Josh hadn't said they wouldn't need to kiss. Just not now. The odds were definitely in his favor that at some point in the weekend he was going to get a bit of lip action.

JOSH TOOK A BITE OF his toast, chewing and swallowing before fastening his gaze on Damian. "Where should we start?"

Damian managed to drag his gaze away from the tanned throat as it contracted. He had to stop staring at him, or he was going to give the game away and then Josh wasn't going to want to be anywhere near him for five minutes, never mind an entire weekend. "I guess, tell me about your family. Particularly those I'm going to be meeting this weekend."

"Erm... my mum and dad will be there, obviously. It's their house. They were childhood sweethearts so they've been married for close to thirty years. It's all very nauseating..." Josh's fond smile said he didn't really feel that way. Damian catalogued the information: close to his mum and dad. "...I have two brothers and two sisters so we're quite a large family. Only my older brother, Mike, and my younger sister, Emily, will be there this weekend, though. Mike's married so his wife will be there too. They've got a two-year-old, who's an absolute bundle of energy, but very sweet."

Damian felt like he should be taking notes. "Girl or boy?"

"Boy. Jamie. My sister's not married, but all my family are paired up so her boyfriend will be there." Josh's eye roll said that he wasn't a huge fan of the boyfriend.

"You don't like him?"

"He's alright. In small doses. He goes by the name Hawk. Which should tell you a little bit about him."

Damian almost choked on his coffee. "Hawk? Does he make porn as well?"

"Not that I know of." Josh pulled a face. "By the way, my parents don't know anything about the work I do with the studio and I want to keep it that way. So whatever you do, don't mention it this weekend."

"Got it. I understand. Mine don't know either." Mind, it was a bit of a different situation for Damian. He'd only been doing it for a few weeks. Josh's performances as Angel spanned almost three years. It must take some doing to keep a secret like that for that length of time. He mimed pulling a zip across his lips.

Josh nodded in recognition of his agreement to keep it a secret. "What about you? I guess I need to know at least a bit about your family."

Damian thought for a moment. "Mum and Dad. Still married." He gave Josh a sunny smile. "I guess that makes us both quite rare. Although, they weren't childhood sweethearts. They got together in their early twenties. I've got one brother who's older. He's a lawyer. They live in Milton Keynes." Damian was struggling to think of anything exciting to say about them. They were just his family. They only needed to know the basics about each other anyway, provided they weren't trying to pretend that they'd been together for ages. "How long are we going to say we've been a couple?"

Deep grooves appeared in Josh's forehead as he contemplated the question. It made Damian want to reach over and smooth them away. "Six months? No, that's too long. Four months. I don't know. What do you think?"

Damian gave it the same consideration. "Three months, maybe? Long enough that it's not too weird that you're introducing me to your parents, but short enough that we're not claiming to have found *the one*." It rankled to say the last bit aloud, but he needed to keep the rational part of his brain functioning, the part that needed to remember that they were only going to be playing at being boyfriends.

"Three months it is." Josh paused to take a sip of his coffee. "How did we meet? That's usually the first question that gets asked so we should definitely be prepared for it."

Damian smiled. "That's easy. You were in a bar with some friends. I spotted you across the room and was immediately smitten. It took me all night to pluck up the courage to approach you, but it was getting late and I knew if I didn't, you'd walk out of my life forever. You were charmed by my bad pickup lines. You thought I was funny... and cute. We talked for an hour and almost forgot that anyone else was there. At the end of the night, you kissed me and asked for my number and we met for coffee the next day. We've been together ever since." Damian broke out of his musings to find Josh staring at him wide-eyed. *Fuck!* He'd gone too far. Got too caught up in the fantasy. At least he hadn't said he'd seen him naked on camera and been drooling over him ever since. He ducked his head and shrugged. "I don't know. Something like that anyway." There was an awkward pause while Damian pretended a fascination in his coffee that the almost empty mug didn't deserve. "I have a vivid imagination."

The hesitation from the man sat opposite him was just that one beat too long. "I guess you would. What with being a drama student. I suppose it comes with the territory."

Right! He'd told him that as well. This was beginning to feel like a lie within a lie, all topped off with a smattering of bullshit. He risked a glance across the table at Josh's expression. At least the initial shock of the fantasy he'd weaved seemed to have worn off somewhat. Now Josh just looked mildly uncomfortable, rather than someone who was one step away from bolting for the nearest exit.

Damian aimed a smile he hoped appeared reassuring and not at all stalker-like in Josh's direction. "What else do we need to go through?"

Chapter Three

JOSH WASN'T QUITE SURE what to make of Damian. The guy didn't seem to fit into any clear category. He went from acting almost shy one minute, to seeming more at ease and cracking jokes the next. It was intriguing. *Which was the real Damian?* For a drama student who made porn on the side, he seemed pretty bad at hiding his reactions, like back in the services when he'd appeared mortified by the complex story he'd woven about their fictional first meeting.

They'd spent the rest of the journey sharing tidbits of information, trying to flesh out their knowledge of each other. It had almost become a competition as to who could come up with the most bizarre category. It had started with music and films and then somehow traveled down the road of most embarrassing moments, and the thing you've never told anyone. It was noticeable that Damian had squirmed out of that question, changing the subject pretty damn fast.

The strange thing was, it had been fun. He'd probably learned more specific information about Damian in the space of a few hours than he'd known about his last boyfriend, even though they'd been together six months. They'd covered that category as well, Damian disclosing that his relationships didn't tend to last longer than a few weeks. Josh found that hard to believe. The guy was cute as a button, a good conversationalist, and funny to boot. He'd make the perfect boyfriend for the right guy. Only, not this weekend. This weekend he was going to be Josh's fake boyfriend. Maybe once the weekend was over, he could help him out, introduce him to one of his friends or something.

Josh brought the car to a halt and stared at the gate they'd parked outside.

Damian shifted in his seat. "What's wrong? Got the wrong house?"

He flicked a sideways look at his travelling companion. "No, just wondering if it's too late to turn around and go back home. The door flew open and his mum came barreling down the path toward the car. "Yep. Way too late. Are you ready for this?"

Damian's sharp intake of breath was easily audible in the confines of the car as he undid his seatbelt and reached for the door handle. "As I'll ever be."

The words weren't that comforting to Josh's ears. If Damian freaked out, then the game would be up before it had even begun. And he'd have an awful lot of explaining to do. *What the hell had he been thinking?* He braced himself and stepped out of the car, where he was immediately swept up into an enthusiastic, perfumed embrace. "Joshy! I've missed you, honey. It's been way too long since you last came home."

He squeezed her tightly. "I know, Mum. I'm sorry, but what with university and everything, I've been busy. I'd never miss your birthday though, you know that." He was dimly aware of Damian coming to stand next to him. It was time to start the charade. Any chance of doing the sensible thing and coming clean was well gone. Josh gave her one last squeeze before levering himself away. "Mum, this is Damian."

She gave a high-pitched squeal, wrapping Damian up in a brief hug before holding him at arm's length so that she could get a good look at him. For once, Josh wasn't surprised by the blush that crept over Damian's features. He should have warned him that his mother wasn't one to stand on ceremony. She turned to face him. "You didn't tell me he was so handsome."

Josh rolled his eyes. "Mum!?"

She shushed him, turning back to Damian whose cheeks were now a bright, fiery red. "Well, he is. I'm not going to pretend he isn't. Let's get you both inside and settled. Emily and Hawk are already here. I figured I'd give you half an hour to freshen up and then we'll have a late lunch. And then I suppose you boys will want to be off somewhere exploring, especially if Damian's never been to Blackpool before."

Josh grabbed the bags out of the back of the car before locking it. He shoved Damian's into his arms. "You make us sound like we're ten."

His mum put her hands on her hips and glared at him, but it was laced with humor. "Would you rather I suggested you might want to be alone? No screwing on the beach. They've been doing patrols. And where's your manners? Your boyfriend's a guest. Why aren't you carrying his bag to your room for him?"

Josh hadn't missed Damian's flinch at the use of the singular for room. Something else that he probably should have warned him about. Luckily, his mum had already turned away so she hadn't caught it. He grabbed hold of Damian's arm. "Follow me." He addressed his mum as they followed her inside. "We'll be as quick as we can and then I'll introduce Damian to everybody." He led him up the path, into the house and straight up the stairs before they could get waylaid by anyone. Then he ushered him into the guest room that used to be his bedroom, waiting for the explosion to hit once the door was closed. It wasn't an explosion though, more a fizzle of confusion as Damian stared at the double bed as if he'd never seen one before.

Damian opened his mouth, closed it again and then finally seemed to muster speech from somewhere. "Room? As in we're both staying in here?" He raised an arm and gestured at the bed. "Both in there? I thought..."

"You thought what?"

His gaze didn't shift from the bed as he answered Josh's question. "It's your parents' house. Surely, they don't approve of... well, you know."

Josh gave in to the smile he'd been attempting to hold back. The guy made porn. How could he kick up such a fuss about having to share a bed? "Didn't you hear my mum make a quip about us screwing on the beach? They're pretty progressive—both of them. They wouldn't dream of making us sleep in separate rooms. It's no biggie. Right?" Damian still hadn't managed to tear his eyes away from the bed. It was like he was transfixed by the sight. Josh gave a small headshake. *Strange guy.* He inclined his head toward the door on the other side of the room. "Bathroom's through there if you want to spend a few minutes freshening up? You can go first." At least that seemed to get through to him, Damian finally dragging himself away from the bed and disappearing through the door.

DAMIAN TOOK AS LONG as he could in the bathroom. The news that he was going to be sharing a bed with Angel/Josh had thrown him for a loop. Not for the reasons Josh was probably thinking, but because he was already trying to work out how he was meant to keep his hands off him when he was going to be lying right next to him half-naked. Maybe even naked. *Oh God! What did Josh sleep in?* A few more hours and Damian would get to find out. What was *he* going to sleep in? He needed something that would hide a permanent erection. Like a suit of armor.

He leaned against the sink, making a concerted effort to calm the butterflies in his stomach. Spending the whole weekend freaking out would be such a waste. This weekend should be fun. After all, Josh was just a man. A sexy, alluring man who made Damian want to lick him all over, but a man nonetheless. He stared at his reflection in the mirror, watching as his lips slowly curled into a smile. Fun! Yeah, that's exactly what this weekend needed to be. As far as he was concerned, for the next forty-eight hours Josh wasn't his fake boyfriend, but his real one. And his performance was going to reflect that. Josh wasn't going to know what had hit him.

He was still smiling when he stepped back out into the bedroom. Josh paused from unpacking his bag to shoot him a quizzical look. "Are you okay?"

Damian nodded slowly, the silent talking-to he'd given himself in the bathroom making him feel like a whole new person. "I'm fine."

Josh scrutinized him for a few seconds, apparently satisfied with what he saw. He gestured toward the chest of drawers. "The bottom two are empty if you want to stash some of your stuff in there. There's space in the wardrobe too if you brought anything you need to hang up." He took a few steps toward the bathroom. "I'll only be a few minutes and then I'll take you to meet the rest of my family."

Bag unpacked—it wasn't like he'd brought a lot of clothes for two days—Damian sat on the edge of the bed and waited for Josh to come out of the bathroom. Once he had, they made their way downstairs, Josh leading the way into the living room where three people stood with smiles on their faces. Josh's dad was easy to recognize: he was an older, but no less handsome version of his son. Josh's sister, Emily, also shared the family resemblance, but in a much more feminine way. The third person looked like he'd just escaped from a motorcycle gang. He was huge, broad, covered in tattoos, and had long hair tied back in a ponytail. Damian supposed that he was good-looking enough, if rough and ready was your type. This had to be Hawk. Now that he'd met him, the name seemed to match, especially given the tattoo on one meaty bicep which depicted exactly that, the curved beak and talons looking especially convincing.

When Josh started making the introductions, Damian decided it was time to start having some fun. He hooked his arm around Josh's shoulder, pulling him in close until their bodies touched, Josh stiffened slightly against him before relaxing into it. Damian leaned in closer still, brushing his lips over Josh's cheekbone before letting his hand drop to rest on the juncture of his back just above his ass. If he was going to get away with touching Josh for two days, then he was going to make the most of it.

It was difficult to concentrate on what was being said when the majority of his attention was focused on the body heat emanating through the thin fabric of Josh's T-shirt. It was untucked. It would be so easy to slip his hand underneath and curl his fingers around his make-believe boyfriend's waistband in order to feel bare skin. And nobody would think anything of it. Well, apart from Josh. But it wasn't as if he'd protest. Not in front of his family anyway. Not unless he wanted to blow the whole thing.

Despite his mind being on far more important things, Damian somehow managed to make all the right noises during the introductions. His fingers slipped lower, the temptation becoming overwhelming. Just a touch. Just long enough to discover if Josh's skin felt as good as it looked on camera. He'd reached the hem of his T-shirt. All he had to do was lift it slightly and then slide his fingers underneath.

"Lunch is ready."

Josh jerked away from him, already stepping toward the door where his mum's raised voice had come from. Damian followed him, finding a large kitchen with the table set up for lunch. He took the seat next to Josh's, moving his chair across slightly so they were closer together, every movement of Josh's arm brushing against his. Hawk took the seat opposite with Josh's sister next to him, while his parents bracketed each end of the table. There was an array of dishes in the center designed for self-service, everything from cold meat to crusty bread, and potato salad.

Josh's mum smiled at him. "Don't stand on ceremony. Dig in. I didn't make it for it not to be eaten. Damian returned her smile before reaching over and starting to fill his plate. "Thanks, Mrs. Keating."

She gave him a mock scornful look. "Oh, please. Call me Miranda. Now, tell me all the juicy information that Josh hasn't bothered to tell us about how you two met."

Damian slid his hand across the table until he could grasp hold of Josh's. He kept hold of it while he reeled off the story he'd fabricated earlier. It seemed less creepy than it had before. Perhaps because by the second telling, he was actually starting to believe it? Damian even added more details, describing what Josh had been wearing the first time he'd ever laid eyes on him. It was completely made up. In reality, the first time he'd ever seen Angel, he'd been as naked as the day he was born. Throughout Damian's story, Josh stayed largely silent, letting him run with it, the hand twitching beneath Damian's the only sign of discomfort.

The good news was that no one questioned it. That was the first huge obstacle out of the way.

Josh waited until Damian had finished talking before lifting their joined hands. "You're going to have to let go. I need both hands to eat."

Damian shot him his best look of pure adoration. And let's be honest, it wasn't difficult when he did actually adore him. "Do you have to eat? You know how much I love to hold your hand."

Josh's smile for his parents was very much at odds with his fingers squeezing Damian's hand just hard enough to cause pain. "He does. He's very affectionate." He rolled his eyes in a "what can you do?" gesture. Then he squeezed a bit harder. Damian let go. When something nudged Damian's leg under the table, he shifted so that his feet were tucked more firmly under it. *Was he taking up too much space?* He frowned as Hawk caught his eye and gave him a broad smile across the expanse of the table. *What was that all about?*

There were more casual questions aimed their way over the next thirty minutes. Luckily, it was all stuff they'd practiced, and Josh managed to interact and give some of the details to the questions that were asked, with Damian confirming them. The only awkward part—for him—was during the discussion of why he'd chosen a degree in drama. He'd had to rack his brain for that one. It was a shame that the vivid imagination he'd claimed to have earlier only seemed to come into operation when it involved Josh.

The potato salad proved particularly tasty so it was a no-brainer that Damian was going to have seconds. Unfortunately, the dish was over by Kenneth's elbow—Josh's dad had also insisted on Damian referring to him by his first name. "Angel, can you pass me the potato salad?" The stillness in Damian's body was reflected by the man next to him, both of them realizing at the same time what he'd just done. *God, he was stupid!* It was only day one. In fact, it was only hour one and he'd already fucked up. He opened his mouth with no idea what to say, but knowing that he had to say something.

Emily let out a loud squeal. "Oh, how cute is that. They've already got pet names for each other. Angel! Isn't that sweet?" She nudged her boyfriend, her elbow barely making a dent in his massive biceps. If he did think it was sweet, he hid it well behind a non-committal grunt. Damian was already getting the fact that Hawk wasn't a big talker. Emily leaned forward, smiling at her brother. "Go on. What do you call him?"

Josh laughed, his gaze flicking toward Damian. "You tell them."

Damian swallowed, his mind going completely blank. Pet names? He couldn't think of a single one. There was only one thing for it—to pass the buck back again. He fluttered his eyelashes. "No, you. After all, you were the one that came up with it. I don't want to steal your thunder."

A muscle ticked in Josh's cheek. "Well, that's easy. He calls me Angel and I call him Leo, because he's my little lion. Cute on the outside but fierce on the inside."

Damian stared at him. It was so obvious; it was genius. Now, both of them would be safe if they slipped up. It would be the perfect time for a kiss. They'd all expect it after the pet names reveal and the sweet—albeit fabricated—reason Josh had just given. He leaned forward slightly, hoping Josh would take the hint. Josh leaned in. It was going to happen. He was going to kiss him. He didn't give a fuck that they had an audience. As far as Damian was concerned it was just the two of them, and this wasn't a fake kiss. It was Josh coming to the realization that he was attracted to the guy he'd brought home to meet his parents.

A firm rub to his calf made Damian break Josh's gaze. And just like that the moment was broken. His legs were tucked under the chair. There was no way on earth it could have been an accident this time. His eyes lifted to meet Hawk's across the table, the man giving him a long, slow wink. *Fuck!* Damian's gaze darted to Emily, but she seemed completely oblivious to what her boyfriend was up to as she chatted to her parents.

It looked like this weekend was going to throw up more challenges than Damian had anticipated. He carefully moved his chair back, leaving a gap between himself and the table without making it too obvious what he was doing.

Chapter Four

JOSH LED THE WAY TOWARD the seafront, his parents happy for him to spend the rest of the day with Damian since the big birthday celebration wasn't until the next day. It was more of a birthday lunch than a dinner in order to leave Josh plenty of time to drive them back to London in the evening.

Today's lunch had been interesting, to say the least. He glanced across at the man ambling along next to him, who'd been virtually silent since they'd left the house. "You were very... er... convincing back there."

Brown eyes settled on him, something stirring in their depths that Josh couldn't identify. Damian shrugged. "Would you rather I hadn't been?"

"No, of course not. I was just surprised that's all. I didn't expect you to throw yourself into it quite that much. But then, I guess you are a drama student, so it probably comes naturally. At one point I was almost convinced myself that we were in a relationship."

Damian laughed, but there was something tinny and artificial about it. "I fucked up though. I called you Angel."

Josh had thought the game was up at that point. Thank fuck for his sister butting in before he'd cracked under the pressure and confessed everything. "Thank God my studio name isn't Wolf or..." He smiled, recalling the name of one of the studio's newest recruits, which provided a perfect example. "...Blaze. We'd never have gotten away with that one."

"I like Angel."

Josh waited for Damian to say more, but nothing else seemed to be forthcoming. "Anyway, they all seemed to buy it so the hardest bit is over. Now, we just need to keep it up and not let our guard down. They all liked you." He smiled wryly. "I guess I know what kind of guy they're hoping I'll bring home in the future."

Damian gave a quiet little huff. Josh couldn't tell whether it was caused by amusement or something else. He was still pondering it when Damian reached across and grabbed his arm, bringing them both to a halt, the brown eyes intent on his face. "What's the story with your sister and Hawk?"

"Story? What do you mean?"

His fake boyfriend looked decidedly uncomfortable, his gaze sliding sideways to focus on a tree. "How long have they been together?"

He considered it, trying to recall what month it was that they'd started seeing each other. "About a year, I think. They had a break-up in the middle of it, but then they got back together within a couple of weeks. Why?"

Damian's teeth bit into his bottom lip, the action firing sudden thoughts in Josh's brain that weren't really appropriate. He fought to keep his mind on the subject under discussion rather than letting it wander off into darker territory. Damian grimaced. "He... was giving me signals all through lunch."

"Signals?" It took a moment for Josh to work out what Damian was getting at. When it finally clicked, he couldn't stop himself from bursting out laughing. "Oh my God! I know you said you had a vivid imagination, but I didn't realize it was that bad. Let me get this straight. Pardon the pun. You're not only accusing him of being bi, or secretly gay, but you're saying he came on to you right in front of his girlfriend and his girlfriend's brother, who he thinks is your boyfriend? Is that what you're saying?" Damian stalked off and Josh had to break into a jog to catch up with him. "Listen, I'm sorry. It just sounds a bit crazy. I'm sure—"

Damian shook his head. "Forget it. Like you said, I probably imagined it. Anyway, where are we going?"

The expression on Damian's face said he didn't think he'd imagined it at all, but Josh decided that it was better to follow his lead and let the subject drop. Where they were going was a good question. He had a soft spot for Blackpool. It was, after all, where he'd grown up. But like most coastal towns, the choices for entertainment were all a bit touristy. Therefore, he wasn't sure how Damian was going to react to his suggestion. For that reason, he braced himself as he made the suggestion. "I thought we could go to the Pleasure Beach if it's not too cheesy? Ride a few roller coasters."

He was surprised by the huge smile that immediately dawned on Damian's face. "Not cheesy at all. Sounds fun. I was hoping we might go. I just didn't want to be the one to suggest it in case you thought I was lame."

Josh winked at him. "Well, let's go and be lame together."

THE PLEASURE BEACH was indeed fun. They'd ridden every ride they could; Damian turned out to be quite the adrenaline junkie who didn't need to be talked into going on any of them. Josh had been surprised at how quickly time had passed as conversation and laughter had flowed freely. To the point that they'd only thought about leaving once the rides had started to gradually close for the evening. He glanced over at his companion, who seemed to be sizing up the best way to tackle the toffee apple he was holding. "You need to open your mouth wider."

Damian's gaze swiveled in his direction and he raised an eyebrow. "I bet you say that to all the boys."

Josh gave him a cheeky wink. "Only the ones I like." There was that little blush again. Not quite as pronounced as it had been earlier, but still there nonetheless. It was quite sweet really. He decided that he needed to flirt with Damian more. See what else made him blush. Or maybe go even further than that? During the last few hours, a germ of an idea had started to manifest itself. Damian was seriously cute and they were stuck together for the next day and a half.

Assuming Damian was willing, why shouldn't they have a bit of fun? It was no different than picking someone up in a bar. Okay, it was a bit different, considering they were already pretending to be in a relationship and were staying at his parents' house, but that didn't need to be too much of a stumbling block, given how free and easy his parents were. And Josh didn't need to be worried about things being awkward at the studio afterward, seeing as his usual routine meant that his path rarely crossed with any of the other models unless he was shooting a scene with them. Damian would be easy enough to avoid, should it come to that.

He was getting ahead of himself though. He needed to gauge if the other man was interested first. "Want to go for a walk on the beach before we head back?"

While Damian considered the question, Josh covertly scrutinized his expression, attempting to work out what he was thinking, but for once Damian was inscrutable. He'd given up on the toffee apple a while ago, its remnants consigned to the bin a few meters back. Finally, Damian nodded. "Sure. Sounds good."

They walked along the seafront until they reached the steps that would take them down onto the beach. After a few minutes of silent strolling, Josh decided it was time to break it. He repeated the words he'd just come up with over and over in his head a few times, trying to ensure they'd sound right when they tumbled from his lips. "By the way, I think you were right earlier. We probably do need to practice the kissing bit."

Damian came to a sudden halt, whirling around to face Josh with a look of surprise on his face. "What made you change your mind?"

The fact that I really want to kiss you and then do a lot more than that. The fact that I might be able to tell how receptive you are to the idea by your response. He couldn't say that. Josh cleared his throat. "You know, the whole 'what happened over lunch' thing. There was a perfect opportunity to kiss, which would have seemed completely natural, and would have helped us to be even more convincing. But we both hesitated. It was just a good job that no one was watching us that closely or they might have worked out what was going on. It'd be a shame to have come this far, and put this much groundwork in, only to fall at the final hurdle."

It was starting to get dark, especially on the beach where there was no lighting. So it was difficult for Josh to be able to tell what Damian was thinking with his expression masked in shadows. He'd been the first one to suggest it, though, back at the service station, so the idea couldn't have been that abhorrent.

Josh's heart gave a strange little thud as Damian came a step closer. He tipped his head back and Josh already knew he was going to say yes before he spoke. Even so, he waited, wanting to know what he'd say. "It would be a shame. I mean, I got your reasoning before about us both making porn. But how many scenes have you shot where you've had to redo the kissing scenes because it wasn't quite right?"

Not many. In fact, Josh was struggling to recall a single occasion. The fucking, yes. Camera angles with legs and arms getting in the way were notoriously difficult. They often had to stop and reset, finding an angle that worked in that position. But kissing was pretty straightforward once you'd gotten into a rhythm. "Oh, loads."

Damian's hands fastened on Josh's shoulders, his fingers curling around them to tug Josh a bit closer. "Exactly. Yeah, we better practice, then. Just a quick one."

Josh slid his arm around Damian's back, flattening his palm and pressing their bodies together until their chests almost touched. He nodded. "Yeah. Better safe than sorry. Practice makes perfect." He was about to go for a third nonsensical cliché, but he didn't get a chance to because Damian was already closing the remaining space between them, his mouth descending to cover Josh's own. It started chastely, just a delicate brush of lips. But that didn't last long. Damian wasted no time in deepening it, and Josh immediately opening up to the questing tongue, meeting it with his own as he tilted his head to find the perfect angle for exploration and to ensure their noses didn't clash. Then he forgot all about the technical aspects, concentrating simply on the touch, taste, and feel of his partner as their mouths got better acquainted.

All thoughts of why they were kissing floated off into the ether as his hands explored Damian's lean back. The fabric underneath his fingertips was frustrating when it was bare skin he wanted. That's what he needed: skin-to-skin contact. Damian's hands slipped downward, moving to grasp Josh's ass. He took it as an invitation to do the same, his fingertips digging into Damian's denim-clad ass, his rapidly swelling cock rubbing against the hard thigh pressed against it. Josh shifted slightly, searching for the evidence that Damian was getting hard too, even as their lips remained fused together. *Bingo! There it was.* They might be faking a relationship, but there was no faking the sexual chemistry they shared. Not when the evidence of it was rapidly growing in their respective trousers.

It was with great reluctance that Josh eventually let go, stepping back to put a bit of space between them. If they let things go on for much longer, they were going to be rutting against each other on a public beach like a pair of randy teenagers. What had seemed at the time like a ludicrous warning from his mum about screwing on the beach was about to come true unless Josh could manage to show a bit of restraint. He needed to say something. Anything.

But words seemed to have become submerged beneath the insistent throbbing in his groin that demanded he throw Damian down on the sand, climb on top of him, and pick up where they'd just left off. "I think... that will probably be fairly convincing."

Damian crossed his arms over his chest and then just as quickly uncrossed them again, letting his hands fall to his sides. "I think so. Although, we might want to avoid the groping bit in front of your parents. It might be slight overkill."

There wasn't a lot Josh could say to that, not without admitting that they'd both gotten a bit carried away. A quick kiss, Damian had said. It wasn't like Josh had timed it, but they had to have been necking on the beach for close to five minutes. He'd have bet his car on it. "We should... probably head back. My parents are going to be wondering where we've gotten to."

Nodding, Damian headed for the closest steps. Josh let his gaze drop to his ass as he followed, annoyed that in the gloom, he couldn't make out that much. If it looked half as good as it had felt nestled in his palms, then it was a very fine ass indeed. He smiled at the realization that they were going to be sharing a bed. And parents or no parents, he intended to make the most of it. His fake boyfriend had better brace himself.

Chapter Five

DAMIAN STARED AT HIS reflection in the bathroom mirror, feeling like a teenage girl in the throes of her first crush. Angel had kissed him. Well, not Angel, Josh. But it was basically the same thing. *Or was it better?* It was better, right? Angel was the fantasy while Josh was the real flesh and blood. Angel was the devilishly sexy man who only let the audience know so much before fucking his scene partner. But Josh. Josh was the man who'd shared snippets of his childhood with Damian this afternoon. Who'd pointed out the school he'd gone to as they'd walked past. Who'd laughed at Damian's jokes no matter how corny they were. Yeah, Josh was a thousand times better. And it was Josh that had kissed him. *Wasn't it?* And it hadn't just been any kiss. It had been one of the best kisses Damian had ever had. He was getting hard again just thinking about it. He could write poetry about that kiss. Or at least he could if he'd ever written poetry in his life.

He took a deep breath, fighting to get things back into perspective. The kiss had been fantastic, but he needed to remember that it had been practice. Just a means of ensuring that their fake relationship went undetected. Only, there'd been nothing fake about the semi-hard cock he'd felt against his thigh. But then, Angel was a pro, right? He'd been making porn for so many years that he could probably snap his fingers and get an erection. Damian needed to ensure that he wasn't spinning one practice kiss into something it wasn't, especially when that man was currently lounging in his underwear on the bed they were about to share.

Damian glanced down. It was lucky that he'd brought sweatpants. Not to wear in bed because he hadn't expected to find himself sharing one with Angel/Josh. But they were certainly going to prove useful in keeping his cock under control. Because right now the organ in question was being far from obedient, due to Damian reliving the kiss on the beach. He stood back from the mirror and turned slightly to the side, trying to ascertain how obvious it was that he was aroused. Thanks to the thick fabric, the answer was not very unless you looked closely. He just needed to make sure that he dived straight beneath the covers after leaving the bathroom.

"Hey, Damian. You okay? You spend more time in the bathroom than my sisters do. Come to bed."

The insult, shouted through the closed bathroom door, didn't even register. All Damian could hear were the last three words. *Come to bed. Come to bed.* They reverberated around his skull, causing his cock, which had calmed down somewhat, to immediately perk up again. He moved closer to the mirror, leaning his hands on the sink, and looking himself straight in the eye. "Keep your hands off him. Don't grope him. Don't cuddle him while he's asleep. Don't even look at him and you'll be fine. You can do that."

Pep talk completed, he took a deep breath before opening the door and walking quickly toward the bed. Josh was propped up against the pillows with his laptop on his knees, bare chest on display. He lifted his head and frowned at Damian. "Are you wearing those to bed? Won't you get hot?"

It was only a few steps to the bed. Damian made them in record time, throwing the covers back and climbing in. He probably would be hot, but he wasn't going to admit that. He was more concerned about keeping his unruly cock under lock and key. "I'll be fine." He lay on his back, staring up at the ceiling, every fiber of his being keenly aware of the body only a few inches away from his. *Now what? Think of something to talk about.* He risked a quick peek at his bed partner. Josh's focus was firmly fixed on the laptop screen in front of him. "Are you working?"

Josh glanced over at him with a smirk. "Nope. Just curious."

Damian wasn't sure whether the words were meant to make sense, but they didn't. Not even slightly. "Curious about what?"

He turned the laptop slightly to the side so that Damian could see the screen. The first thing he noticed was the familiar *EagerBoyz* banner at the top of the screen, the black background and purple typography making it immediately recognizable. The second thing was the particular page that Josh was on. Damian's profile page as Leo Stone. The professional shot the studio had taken of Damian filled one corner of the screen while the few scenes he'd shot for them were listed underneath. A surge of panic shot through him, turning his blood to fire. He sat up, making a lunge for the laptop. Josh was faster, moving it away before he could get hold of it, Damian's fingers barely brushing it before it was out of reach. It meant that instead of managing to wrestle the laptop from Josh, he ended up sprawled in his lap instead.

Josh raised an eyebrow as he looked down at him. His lips curled up into that familiar smile, the dimples appearing in his cheeks. "Hey, down there. You comfortable?"

Cheeks burning, Damian scrambled back to his own side of the bed, watching with narrowed eyes as Josh pulled the laptop back onto his lap and started inputting the free login password they were all given—one of the perks of filming for them. "What are you doing? You can't watch that."

Josh lifted his index finger in the air and made a big show out of pressing return, the screen changing from the free previews to the actual videos. "Why can't I? They're in the public domain. I hate to tell you this, but if you didn't want anyone to see them, the internet's not really the best place."

Damian wasn't having that. "You know exactly what I mean. You can't watch it while I'm here. That's weird. How would you like it if I watched one of your scenes?"

"We'll watch one of mine next. Just be patient."

Damian almost swallowed his tongue. This couldn't be happening. Any moment now, he'd wake up and realize that he'd fallen asleep as soon as his head had touched the pillow and everything after that had been some sort of weird dream, manifested by his brain going haywire over a kiss.

The cursor hovered over each of the videos one by one while Josh considered his options. "Not interested in your solo. No offence. And blow jobs aren't really my thing unless I'm giving or receiving one so we can give that one a miss as well. So that leaves us a choice of three. Any preference?"

What was he supposed to say to that? Although actually, he did have a sort of preference. Anything but the very first one he'd made, where despite Evan assuring him it was fine, Damian still saw traces of rabbit caught in the headlights, rather than slick performer. He was about to say that but the cursor was already moving across the screen, Josh announcing "this one" and clicking on a video that he'd filmed a few weeks ago. Josh shot Damian a quick glance. "You filmed with Ryker. He's pretty good. I did a scene with him once."

The words "I know" hovered on Damian's tongue before he bit them back. It was one of his favorite scenes of Angel's, guaranteed to get him off in record time. Ryker was pale-skinned and blond. The difference between Angel's darker skin and Ryker's paler complexion, not to mention Ryker's incredible enthusiasm at getting fucked by Angel, his hands continually roving all over his body, had made it hot with a capital H. Damian said nothing, watching in trepidation as Josh pressed play. He paused it after a couple of seconds, reaching across to the nightstand for the headphones he used with his phone and plugging them in. Damian shook his head as he was offered one of the earbuds. Josh shrugged and placed both of them in his own ears.

There was no way that Damian could bring himself to look at the screen. If he did, there was a danger of him spontaneously combusting from embarrassment. So he watched Josh instead, concentrating on being able to look his fill while Josh's focus was elsewhere. Damian calculated that at the moment the video was still on the talking part. He tried to remember what he'd said. What were the questions Evan had asked that day? Something about favorite sexual positions. He tried to remember what his answer had been but drew a blank.

Josh let out a snort of laughter. Damian's eyes flicked to his face. He still couldn't bring himself to look at the screen. "What?"

"Your favorite sexual position is whichever one means you can get your dick in the quickest. Nice answer. You're funny on camera as well."

Right. That's what he'd said. Mainly to avoid a long conversation so that they could get on with filming the scene. He'd had an exam that day that he'd needed to study for so he'd been hoping to keep filming time down to a couple of hours. Damian tried to recall how long the scene was once it had been edited to within an inch of its life. About twenty-five minutes as far as he could remember. Josh wouldn't watch it all, surely? The minutes ticked by. The "action" had to have started by now. Was it turning Josh on? It had to be, right? That was the whole purpose of porn. Why else would he be watching it? This situation was a complete mind-fuck. He closed his eyes, wondering whether he could manage to fall asleep. Unconsciousness sounded like a perfect way to escape.

"You need to think more about where your hands are when you're filming."

Damian's eyes snapped open to find Josh peering at the screen with a slight furrow to his brow. "You're critiquing me?"

Josh gave a slight shrug. "Just trying to help you improve. I mean, look at this." Against his will, Damian did look, watching the him on screen roll about on the bed with the smaller blond man, both of them naked. The only good thing was that because they were plastered together, Damian's cock wasn't on display. Not yet, anyway.

Tapping the screen, Josh looked Damian's way. "What's that hand doing?"

Damian propped himself up on one elbow, leaning in to get a better look. The hand in question was resting on his scene partner's ass as they kissed. "Nothing."

Josh made a tutting sound. "Exactly. What could it be doing?"

"I don't know, Mr. Expert. You tell me."

He turned with a grin. "The answer is anything. *Anything* would be more interesting than it just lying there like a dead fish. You want the audience to believe that you're really into the other guy, whether you are or not. Think about the small things. That's what separates the average guys from the ones that are good at it."

Like you? Damian didn't say it though. He guessed there were worse people to take performance advice from than the darling of the studio, the one who had the record number of subscribers flocking to every video he made—Damian included. Damian had always assumed Angel's performances came naturally. But going by what Josh had just said, they didn't. He put a lot of thought into it.

Josh clicked on the bottom bar of the video, skipping forward a good ten minutes, and Damian was suddenly faced with his ass filling the screen as he fucked Ryker. His cheeks flamed again, yet for some reason he couldn't drag his eyes away from the screen this time. His voice when he managed to produce sound came out in a husky whisper. "Going to critique this as well?"

"Nothing to critique. Your on-screen fucking is a lot better than your on-screen foreplay. You make great noises as well."

A jolt of electricity shot through Damian's body. Half arousal, half twisted pride. He went back to watching Josh, noting the flared nostrils and the slight flush of color along his cheekbones. Oh God! He was aroused. Damian's gaze automatically dropped to Josh's crotch, but it was covered by the laptop. He seemed completely oblivious to the fact that Damian was watching him rather than his own performance on the screen. At one point, Josh's hand, which had been resting on his abdomen, began to slide beneath the covers. Damian held his breath. Was he going to get his cock out and start stroking it? Treat him to a live solo performance? If so, Damian was completely on board for that. At the last moment, Josh seemed to catch himself, his hand stalling before returning to where it had started. Damian's disappointment knew no bounds.

Finally, the scene came to an end. There was a moment of stillness between them, Damian balancing on the precipice of feigning sleep or triggering something else entirely. Something that would be far more exciting. Given that his dick had stolen all the blood from his brain though, the decision was a no-brainer. "So... you said we'd watch one of yours next."

Blue eyes settled on him, Josh's cheeks still bearing the flush of arousal. "Sure, but you have to come here and watch it with me."

Come here. There was less than a foot of space between them. Damian didn't say that. Instead he obediently wriggled closer, Josh lifting his arm and then draping it around him once he was in position. And what a position it was, the side of his chest touching Josh's. Damian was surrounded by Josh's smell and touch, the sensations making him dizzy with desire. It was all he could do to remember how to breathe. The arm wrapped around him tightened momentarily. "Relax."

That was easy for him to say. He wasn't pressed up against the guy who'd been the subject of his wank fantasies for the last three years. Damian made an effort to play it cool, feigning relaxation to the best of his ability as he watched Josh navigate the way to his own profile page. Or at least the first one, considering the sheer number of videos he had on the site.

"Have you ever watched any of mine?"

All of them. Multiple times over. I could probably recite the small sections of dialogue by heart. "Some."

"Yeah?"

The surprise in Josh's voice was somewhat of a comfort. It meant that he hadn't picked up on the fact that Damian was completely gaga over him. "Yeah, I mean. I had to research studios before I decided which one to apply for. Best way to do that was to watch some of the videos on offer." His reasoning sounded strangely plausible for a complete lie that had been invented off the top of his head.

Josh nodded, gesturing at the screen with his free hand. "Which one do you want to watch?"

"You choose." Damian grabbed his hand before he could click on anything. "What about your parents?" Both of them knew that the question wasn't about the porn-watching, but the likelihood of what it would lead to. At least Damian hoped it would, because his cock was already hard enough to hammer a nail into wood.

Josh smiled. "They'll both be asleep by now. And trust me, they sleep like the dead. There's no waking them. Emily's gone to stay at Hawk's tonight so that's not an issue either."

Damian relinquished his hand and Josh started the video playing. It was a good choice. It was a scene Angel had filmed with a young redhead, who went by the name Tommy. He'd left the studio way before Damian had ever started filming there. Shame really. He wouldn't have minded a chance to get up close and personal with the hundreds of freckles that covered Tommy's body. It wasn't his favorite scene of Angel's, but it would definitely have ranked somewhere in the top five.

This time when Josh offered him one of his earbuds, he accepted. It started off the same way that all the videos did—with a few minutes of chat, Evan asking Tommy how it felt to be filming a video with Angel. Given the way the redhead was virtually bouncing up and down with enthusiasm as he spoke, none of his exuberant answers were a lie. The usual tinge of jealousy that Damian felt was somewhat muted by the arm around his neck, Josh's fingers softly stroking the hair at the nape of his neck. "Why did you pick this one?"

Josh shrugged. "I don't know. I guess it was one of the more memorable ones to film. Tommy was cute. Also, there's the fact that he comes twice during the video." He waggled his eyebrows. "I always think that's a great advertisement of my... skills."

"You could just as easily have picked your scenes with Logan or Phoenix, then. They both came twice as well." Damian winced, realizing his mistake as soon as the words had left his mouth. *Fucking great!* He'd just revealed himself as a walking encyclopedia of everything Angel-related. He may as well reel off the exact timings of Angel's cum shots in every scene he'd ever filmed. Not that he could. Not for all of his videos anyway.

If Josh had picked up on it, much to Damian's relief he didn't question it. He gave another shrug. "True."

On screen, Tommy was talking about how much he was looking forward to getting fucked by Angel, his fingers edging across the bed toward Angel's thigh, the underwear he was wearing starting to strain at the front. It acted as a trigger in the video, Angel flipping his scene partner onto his back to kiss him, his hands roving all over his body until one finally dipped below the waistband of Tommy's underwear. The camera zoomed in as Angel palmed the prize he'd found beneath the fabric, tracing its shape and squeezing until Tommy moaned, before pulling his underwear down completely and releasing his scene partner's stiff cock. He kissed his way down the freckle-covered body until he took Tommy's dick in his mouth, the camera focusing on the blissed-out expression on Tommy's face before panning to a close-up of Angel's, his cheeks hollowed as he slid his lips off his cock before engulfing it once again.

Damian had lost the ability to breathe. He was suddenly intensely aware of every part of his body that touched Josh's from the fingers in his hair to the curve of his shoulder nestled into the other man's chest. There was enough heat radiating between the two of them to put the sheets at risk of spontaneously combusting. The sweatpants he'd chosen to wear were too thick, too constricting. At least they were keeping his throbbing cock in check, though, so perhaps they had their use. His fingers tightened on the sheet even while he tried to feign relaxation in the rest of his body. He wanted Angel's lips on *his* cock, wanted the ecstasy written over Tommy's face, even if some of it was manufactured for the camera, to be his firsthand experience.

The scene changed in the video, Tommy scrambling to his hands and knees, his pert ass pushed in the air and his slim thighs parted. He looked back over his shoulder, begging Angel to fuck him in a husky voice. In the way that only porn edits could manage, Angel was ready to do exactly that within seconds, condom already on and lubed. Prep would have been done off-camera, leaving Angel with nothing else to do except drag his partner back against him and slowly push his cock inside.

Knowledge of what came next, having watched it a hundred times, didn't make it any less hot. As soon as Angel had lodged himself balls deep inside Tommy, the other man let out a shout, his body trembling as he came hands-free, his cock spurting all over the bed. After a brief expression of surprise, Angel laughed, giving Tommy a few moments to ride through his orgasm before starting to fuck him in earnest.

There were questions Damian would have liked to ask. Questions that always buzzed around his brain whenever he watched this scene. Was the surprise on both men's faces genuine? Or had it been scripted? Assuming it was genuine, had Evan been pleased at the spontaneity of the scene, or pissed that they'd gone off script? From working with the studio boss, Damian couldn't imagine the man being too pleased if *he* came at any other time than the one specified. But then, if the results were so hot, would you complain?

Yeah, he had questions. But voicing them meant creating words, and Damian wasn't currently capable. Not when his body vibrated with desire and longing. At some point he'd moved closer to Josh, so close, they shared the same air, both men's breaths noticeably faster than normal.

Damian kept his eyes fixed on the screen. They'd changed position again, Tommy lying on his back, and holding his legs up by his ears as Angel held a perfect push-up position to plow into the man beneath him, both of them moaning loudly in perfect unison. Damian swallowed, his hand inching across the sheet. He paused. What if he'd gotten this all wrong? What if Josh just had a secret porn-watching kink, but that's all it was? He shifted slightly, the hairs on Josh's arm sliding against his skin and causing goosebumps. God, he was horny. Damian needed to do something, even if that thing was run away to the bathroom and take matters into his own hands, or hand to be more exact.

He was on the brink of putting that plan into action when strong fingers clutched hold of his hand, tugging it beneath the surface of the sheet. Damian held his breath, letting his hand be led. There was the smoothness of taut skin, his digits skating over Josh's perfect abdominals, and then the brush of the thin fabric of Josh's underwear beneath his knuckles.

On screen, Tommy was facedown on the bed, his moans coinciding with every thrust of Angel's cock into his ass. It was becoming harder and harder to care what was happening on screen, when Damian's fingers were in touching distance of the same appendage that was currently driving Tommy toward the second of his two orgasms.

Josh tugged harder, Damian's fingers sliding beneath the fabric of Josh's underwear, the springy texture of pubic hair beneath his palm. And then his hand was guided around a very stiff cock. A rush of heat hit Damian full force. Having guided him there, Josh let go, his hand reappearing above the covers and making it very clear that the choice of whether Damian's hand remained there, was very much his. In Damian's mind, there was no choice. It would have been easier to jump off a high building than to force himself to relinquish his grip on Josh's cock. He wrapped his fingers more firmly around it, giving it an experimental stroke. Josh's hips jerked upward, pushing his cock more firmly into Damian's hand, his breath hot against his ear.

Damian timed his strokes with the action on-screen, trying to match the speed of the fucking. Angel's louder moans on-screen, mixing with the much quieter gasps of the man next to him. Same man. Two different reactions. Did that mean something? Was this real? Or just another performance missing a camera?

It was strange that they hadn't looked at each other once since the video had started. Damian tore his eyes away from the screen, turning his head and fastening his mouth on the hot skin of Josh's neck. He kept up the movement of his hand as he tasted the salty skin. It was like his action had released some sort of dam. Perhaps Damian taking some sort of initiative had been what Josh was waiting for. Whatever it was, Josh's fingers tangled in Damian's hair, tugging his head away from his neck. Damian's lips pursed, ready to protest. He'd finally gotten to taste. He wasn't ready to relinquish his prize yet. Thoughts of protest were stilled, though, when Josh's mouth angled over his. Hot. Needy. Persistent. And so fucking good. They kissed long and hard, the cacophony of moans coming through the single earbud they both still wore nothing but background noise.

Damian tried to get closer, his hand slipping off Josh's dick as he made an attempt to twist his body around to face him. He swore, his attempt foiled by two things: the fact that he was still attached to Josh by the cord of the headphones and the laptop in the way of where he wanted to be. Josh's blue eyes sparkled with amusement and he laughed before plucking the earbud from his own ear, then doing the same to Damian's. He sat up, grabbing the laptop and leaning over the side of the bed to deposit it on the floor before ripping the covers off his side of the bed and lying back, his stiff cock protruding from the underwear bunched around his hips. "Come here."

Straddling Josh's thighs, Damian stared down at the man he adored, trying not to let it show on his face. What he'd felt prior to the weekend had only grown by virtue of getting to know him. They might not have spent that long together, but the hours where it had just been the two of them were long enough for more than lust to have grown. Enjoying his company as well was a dangerous mixture. A mixture that had his heart thumping faster, anticipation at what they were about to do burning through his veins. He needed out of the sweatpants. The clothing chosen to hide a multitude of sins was now nothing more than a prison.

How far were they going to take this? Mutual hand jobs? Blow jobs? Further? His heart jolted. Were they going to fuck? He'd probably have sold his left kidney at that moment for the possibility of that fantasy coming true. Why shouldn't they? All he had to do was open his mouth and say what he wanted. He'd kick himself if he looked back at this weekend, only to realize what a wasted opportunity it had been. How could he phrase it delicately?

"Can we fuck?" Okay. That hadn't been delicate at all. Not even slightly. Damian held his breath, waiting for Josh's response to the blunt question.

Josh cocked his head to the side, looking thoughtful. "Depends."

Damian smoothed his hands over Josh's abdomen, unable to refrain from touching any longer. He traced each muscle. What sort of workout routine did you need in order to get definition like that? "On what?"

The hesitation in Josh's response made Damian drag his eyes away from Josh's six-pack and back to his face. Josh smiled. "Why do you think I chose that particular video of yours? What makes it different to the other scenes you've done?"

Damian thought about it as his hand strayed closer to Angel's cock. He wanted to taste it. Wanted to feel it nudging the back of his throat. What was he meant to be doing? Right. Josh had asked him a question. The least he could do was manage to keep his mind off Josh's cock long enough to make an educated guess at the answer. What *was* different about it? One thing did spring to mind, but he had to be wrong because that didn't make any sense. In the absence of anything better to say, he went with it anyway. "The fact that I topped?"

Josh nodded and Damian frowned. "What's that got to do with anything?" Something clicked into place in his brain. "Oh! That doesn't make sense, though. You've never bottomed on camera." There he went again, revealing that he knew far too much about Angel. It was just Josh who was apparently more difficult to fathom.

"What I do on camera and what I do in real life are two very different things."

A buzz of jubilation shot through Damian, the confirmation that Josh wasn't treating this as a porn scene minus a cameraman was a potent aphrodisiac. Not that he needed one. He was already one hundred percent ready to go. "I see."

Josh's hands smoothed along Damian's thighs, plucking at the thick fabric of the sweatpants. "It's not that I won't. It's just that I prefer bottoming to topping. And"—his lips curled up into a smile, his dimples appearing—"you seemed to be doing a pretty good job of it from what I could see. Is it a problem?"

Damian waited all of one second before shaking his head. He'd have loved to get fucked by Josh, but there was an equal allure to fucking him too. He'd take him any way he could have him. He was versatile anyway. It was just that on camera, Evan seemed to prefer Leo to bottom. So far, anyway. "Do you have condoms?"

Lifting his head off the pillow, Josh gestured over to the chest of drawers where he'd left his wallet on top. He winked. "In there. Seeing as you're on top in more ways than one, why don't you get them. Perhaps you can lose your clothes on the way back. After all..." He pointed toward the abandoned laptop. "I've already seen you naked."

Going through someone else's wallet even with permission felt odd. It was lucky, then, that the need to find condoms and lube far outweighed the need to be polite. Damian quickly found both. He turned back to find a naked Josh waiting for him on the bed. Shedding his sweatpants and underwear in record time, he joined him.

Chapter Six

SHOULD JOSH FEEL GUILTY? Switching the porn on had been blatant manipulation to get Damian in the mood. The way he'd come out of the bathroom, though, wearing almost as much as he had during the day, had almost convinced Josh it wouldn't work.

But work it had.

And when the net result was a naked and aroused Damian who'd agreed to fuck him, it was difficult to muster any negative emotions, never mind guilt. It wasn't like he'd twisted his arm either. After the initial surprise—which was understandable given Angel's default role on screen—Damian had seemed only too keen.

He let his gaze rove all over the other man as he made his way back to the bed. He might have looked his fill when he'd watched Damian's performance as Leo on-screen, but that paled in comparison to the real thing. He might not be as muscular as Josh himself was, but everything was definitely well put together and in perfect proportions. Including his cock.

It was easy to see why Evan wanted Leo topping as well as bottoming. A great ass and a great cock shouldn't be wasted. At least that's what Evan always told Josh when he was trying to get him to relax his stance on bottoming on camera. But Josh wanted to keep something for himself. He did everything else on camera. Getting fucked was his and his alone, and he intended to keep it that way.

As Damian made to climb back onto the bed, Josh stilled him with a hand on his hip, taking the lube and condoms from him, before pulling him closer. He let his hand slide around the back, palming one firm ass cheek, his mouth hovering a few millimeters away from the mouthwatering cock. He glanced up at Damian's face. "Do you mind?"

Damian laughed, his eyebrows rising. "Mind! I'd mind more if you didn't. As long as I get to reciprocate."

Josh had no problem with that. No problem at all. He didn't intend to blow Damian for long, wanting to get to the fucking as quickly as he could after the porn-prolonged foreplay. But it would have been an absolute fucking travesty not to get to taste. Cum might not be his thing but he had no problem with the bit before that. And given the little quivers that ran through Damian's body as Josh swirled his tongue over the sensitive head before taking him deep, it would have been a shame not to get to experience his reactions. Josh was good at blow jobs. Of course he was. He gave them for a living. But they were always so different off camera. It was much more enjoyable when you didn't have to worry about the angle your head was at and whether you were blocking the camera's view. Not to mention when you knew that your partner's reactions weren't staged. Only problem was that he was reluctant to stop in order to give Damian his turn. There was an easy fix for that, though.

He pulled his mouth off Damian's cock with a loud pop, tapping him gently on the ass. "On the bed." Josh used his hands to turn Damian the way he wanted him, until the other man recognized his intention and was only too happy to shift around so they had perfect access to each other's cocks. The new position gave Josh the perfect opportunity to explore Damian's ass while he sucked him. Even better, every little moan he forced from the other man's mouth vibrated down the length of his cock as Damian took him down his throat. It made Josh get even more inventive, just to see what rewards he could get from driving Damian to greater heights of sensation.

Only when they were both in danger of coming, bringing the prospect of them not getting to the fucking, did they both stop. Damian reached for the condom Josh had left by the pillow, Josh laughing as Damian struggled to get it on while seeming unwilling to take his eyes off Josh. So much for them both being seasoned porn performers. "Want me to do it?"

Looking sheepish, Damian finally glanced down, managing to roll the thin layer of latex over his shaft. "I'm so hard. If you're hoping this is going to last a long time, then I'm afraid you're going to be disappointed."

Josh pulled him down for a quick kiss. "Quick and hard works for me." He wasn't lying. Having Damian's throat convulsing around his cock, not to mention his tongue swirling around his sensitive glans, had pushed him to the brink. Unless they took a break, which neither of them seemed inclined to do, then it wasn't going to take too much stimulation of his prostate to push him over the edge.

Damian reached for the lube, squeezing a generous amount onto his palm before smoothing it over his thick cock. Josh was looking forward to being stretched open by it. In the video, Ryker had certainly seemed to be enjoying it. Josh held his hand out for some, rubbing his fingers together as Damian obliged. He hitched his knees up, pushing a lubed finger inside his hole and laughing as Damian nearly swallowed his tongue. "Are you alright?"

"Yeah... just, you know, this is new. Not in the videos."

How many of his videos had Damian watched? He was beginning to think it was a few more than he was letting on, which begged the question why he was being so cagey about it. Now wasn't the time to ask. Now was the time to get fucked by the cute hottie crouching over him, waiting for his signal that he was stretched enough to take his cock. He inserted another finger, his eyes fixed on Damian's face, drinking in his expression. Damian was oblivious, his attention firmly focused on what Josh's fingers were up to.

Damian finally seemed to shake himself from the stupor, his gaze moving upward. "How do you want to do this?"

Josh pushed his fingers deeper, moaning as they brushed his prostate. "One position. No worrying about angles. No one shouting cut or telling me not to come yet. Anything other than that and I'm good." Just as he'd known he would, Damian chuckled. It was refreshing to have sex with someone who got the difference between sex on-screen and sex in real life. Why had he spent years being so adamant not to mix business with pleasure? It seemed he'd been missing out.

He withdrew his fingers, tugging Damian over to him. "Come on, boyfriend. Show me what you've got."

Damian went still. Almost like they'd been playing the video and Josh had pressed pause. Josh frowned. "What did I say?" His confusion didn't clear as Damian ducked his head, hiding his expression from Josh's scrutiny. *What was going on? What had he said wrong?* A few seconds, though, and Damian lifted his head again, all traces of whatever had been bothering him gone. In its place was the cheeky smile he'd worn earlier in the day when he'd so enjoyed playing up to their charade during lunch. He shook his head, knee-walking closer before pushing Josh's thighs wider apart and lining up the head of his cock with his hole.

Josh lay back, putting his hands behind his head, and closing his eyes. He loved that initial stretch, that feeling that was half pleasure and half pain. He was also a fan of lying back and letting the other person take charge. He'd seen it in some of his scene partners, the satisfaction on their faces almost making him jealous when he was playing the other role.

Damian's cock nudged his hole, demanding entrance. Then the head was inside. Hands smoothed over his abs, moving up to tweak one nipple while Damian gave him time to adjust to the initial intrusion. Just a few seconds. No more. No less. And then the thick cock in his ass was being pushed deeper until Josh felt deliciously full. A hand brushed over his cheekbone and he opened his eyes to find himself looking into Damian's face as the man leaned over him. Damian smiled, a smug self-satisfied smile. "You look happy."

He batted Damian's hand away. "Alright, stud. You may have passed the first test. But..." He wiggled his hips experimentally, sparks of sensation shooting down his spine. "There's not a lot going on now. Time to make it interesting. Then you'll make me really happy."

Bracing himself on his elbows, Damian winked. "Challenge accepted." His lips found Josh's as he started to thrust, Josh losing himself to the dual pleasure of kissing while Damian's cock continued to nudge his prostate, each glide over the sensitive bundle of nerves feeling better than the last. He definitely knew what he was doing. Evan should have him top more. Or maybe he shouldn't. Maybe Josh should keep it just for him. Which was a ridiculous thought to have when the whole weekend was make-believe.

Smoothing his hands along Damian's back, Josh bucked his hips up, wanting to feel the other man come in his ass. That was another thing where porn differed. All those wasted cum shots done solely for the camera. Even as a top, Josh hated it. It was the worst part of the job. That moment where you were on the brink of a really good orgasm and then you had to stop, pull out, get rid of the condom and finish by hand on whatever pre-arranged place had been decided before they'd even started filming.

Damian tore his lips away from Josh's, his breathing coming in ragged pants. Then he was thrusting deep, the muscles beneath Josh's hands rigid as he came with a groan. It was enough to trigger the orgasm that Josh had been desperately holding back, his cock sliding against Damian's abdominals as he gave in to it, painting the other man's torso.

He didn't care when Damian collapsed on top of him, welcoming the weight pinning him to the bed and the hot breath in his ear.

Damian exhaled, long and slow. "That was *so* good." He struggled back up to his elbows, lifting his torso slightly to view the evidence of Josh's orgasm, the smug smile returning.

If he'd been feeling less soporific, Josh might have been obliged to be a bit more circumspect, but fresh from coming so hard, his words were as loose as his body. "It was. I think you're probably the best fake boyfriend I've ever had."

Damian let his head drop onto Josh's shoulder. "How many have you had?"

"Just the one. Including you."

"Not much competition, then."

Josh rolled them slightly, keeping Damian in his arms. He wasn't ready to let go of him yet. "True."

Chapter Seven

DAMIAN WAS FLOATING on air and no matter how much his brain kept telling him to calm down and not read too much into the fact that he'd had hot and passionate sex with the man of his dreams, he couldn't force himself to listen to it. And it hadn't just been the once either. When he'd been woken midway through the night by Josh's lips on his neck, closely followed by his hand wrapping around his cock to tease him to hardness, it had taken little to no coercion before he'd found himself buried in Josh's delectable ass once again, both of them taking longer to come this time.

It didn't mean anything. Not really. They both made porn in their spare time, so it wasn't like either of them were averse to casual sex. But that didn't seem to stop Damian's mind from fixating on how Josh had called him his boyfriend and from weaving elaborate fantasies linked to it. Even if he had ruined it later by adding the tag fake to it. Damian's brain was choosing to remember the former and wipe the latter from his memory banks.

Had Josh's parents heard them? Damian had been only too eager to accept Josh's assurances the previous night that they were asleep. But in the cold light of day, when he was thinking with his big head instead of the small one, it was easy to see that there was no way Josh could have possibly known that for sure. *Had they been loud?* He didn't think so. And such was his euphoria that he was finding it difficult to care if they'd heard. Besides, even if they had, it wasn't likely they were going to bring it up.

It didn't stop him from studying them when they appeared for breakfast, searching for any slight signs of embarrassment. There weren't any that he could glean, so either they were just as progressive as Josh had said they were, or they really had been asleep. Breakfast was uneventful with just the four of them, the big birthday lunch for Josh's mum due to occur later at a restaurant where they were going to meet the rest of the family.

This morning, there was nothing feigned about all the little touches Damian managed to sneak in. After all, it was likely that after today, he wasn't going to get a chance again. So any opportunity he could, he cuddled up to Josh, laying his head on his shoulder or touching his arm or his thigh. Once he even leaned in for a kiss, pleased when Josh didn't hesitate to reciprocate. But then, of course he wouldn't. Not in front of his parents anyway.

The restaurant turned out to be a little family-run Italian place tucked away in the backstreets of Blackpool. One of those places that it was difficult to find unless you already had prior knowledge of it, which probably accounted for the fact that there were few people there. They were shown to the table where everyone else was already waiting. A man who looked to be in his late twenties stood up from the table as they approached, his hand outstretched. He was like an older, slightly less good-looking—at least in Damian's opinion—version of his younger brother. "You must be Josh's boyfriend. I'm Mike."

"Damian." He held his hand out, shaking Josh's brother's hand before being introduced to his wife, Camilla. There was no toddler today, the two of them having gotten a sitter. Emily and Hawk were already seated. Much to Damian's consternation, he found himself sandwiched between Josh and Hawk. Josh, he was fine with. But sitting that close to Hawk after his suspicions yesterday, he was less keen about. Josh might have brushed off his allegations, but Damian was still convinced that Hawk's touches had been far from accidental and had been a way of him expressing interest in Damian. What the big, hairy biker guy thought Damian was going to do with that information, with Hawk's girlfriend less than a meter away, he had no idea. But it was still enough to make him feel decidedly uncomfortable as he sat down, deliberately avoiding meeting Hawk's eye.

Trying to be covert about it, Damian shuffled his chair closer to Josh's. Not only did it move him away from Hawk's side, but it had the added bonus of pressing him up against Josh, the heat of the other man's body burning into his side and triggering a memory of pressing up against him without any clothes in the way.

Probably wondering why Damian was suddenly so close, Josh turned with a frown. "Are you okay?"

Damian nodded. There was no point in sharing his concerns when Josh had already dismissed them. Besides, he was being ridiculous. There were eight of them around the table. What was Hawk going to do? Try and cop a feel while everyone was there? Anyway, it wasn't as if Damian was a shrinking virgin. He could handle one guy. The only problem was that should Hawk try anything, Damian didn't want to cause a scene. Josh wouldn't thank him for it. Not when they were there to celebrate Josh's mum's birthday. He forced a smile. "I'm fine. Did you say we're doing presents before we eat?"

Josh's brow furrowed. "Yeah, why?"

"Oh, I brought a little something for your mum. I just wanted to check when the right time to give it to her was."

Josh's eyebrows shot up. "You did!?" He'd made no move to put any distance between them so the two of them were still sharing the same space.

Damian took a moment to remind his unruly cock that Josh was only tolerating it for appearance's sake. He wouldn't be snuggling with him if it was only the two of them. "It seemed like a nice thing to do."

The sexy fucking dimples appeared as Josh smiled. As usual, it had a profound effect on Damian, making his palms sweaty, his heart speed up, and his cock throb all at the same time. "That's really sweet of you."

Damian shrugged, pulling the small, wrapped box out of his pocket, and passing it over the table. "Mrs. Keating. Sorry, I mean Miranda. Happy birthday. This is just a little something I picked up for you."

She beamed at him, taking it from him and immediately ripping the paper open before removing the box lid. "Oh, that's lovely!" She turned the box around, holding it up so that everyone could see what it contained. "Look, everyone. Damian got me a gorgeous brooch for my birthday. Isn't that pretty?" She turned her attention to Josh, leaning forward and speaking in an exaggerated stage-whisper. "You need to hang on to this one for longer than five minutes. He's handsome *and* thoughtful."

Damian blushed, his cheeks flaming even more as Josh turned his head, giving him a look full of what could only be described as fondness and uttering the words, "I know," in a husky whisper. He leaned over, not that he had far to go when they were still crushed together, his lips on course for Damian's cheek. *Just an act, Damian. Just an act. Don't get too excited.* It didn't stop him from turning his head, so that instead of Josh's lips brushing his cheek, their lips met instead. The resulting kiss, which should have been brief, turned into much more, the two of them only breaking apart at Mike's pointed cough. *Fuck!* Everyone was staring at them. At him. Damian ducked his head. "Sorry."

Emily laughed. "You don't need to apologize for being completely gaga over my brother. It's nice to see him picking someone decent for once. He used to have terrible taste in men. What was the name of that guy, Josh, the one you were dating just after you left school, before you moved to London?"

Josh shook his head. "I don't know who you're talking about." His hand wandered across to Damian's thigh and gave it a squeeze, the action causing a frisson of desire to pass through Damian's body. He was even happier when he left it there.

Tutting, Emily raised her eyes to the ceiling. "Yes, you do. You just don't want to admit what terrible taste you had in front of your boyfriend. The one that had dyed his hair blue but it kept coming off on his skin so he looked like a Smurf, and he wore a fake nose ring because his parents wouldn't allow him to get it done for real. That one. What was his name?"

Josh looked like he was trying to be serious for a moment, but then his lips quirked. He paused for a moment as his mum opened the present from him and leaned over the table to give him a kiss on the cheek as thanks. "Do you mean his real name, or the one he'd changed it to and demanded everyone call him?"

Banging her hand on the table, Emily looked delighted. "That's right. I remember now. Martin by day. Orb by night."

"Orb!" Damian couldn't help but repeat the word. "You dated a man who looked like a Smurf and called himself Orb?"

Narrowing his eyes, Josh gave his sister a mock-glare. "Thanks for the reminder and for telling Damian all about it."

She wrinkled her nose. "You're welcome. I just thought I'd let him know how little competition there was in your past relationships."

Damian appreciated it, even if it did make him feel guilty for misleading her when competition was hardly the biggest issue in his non-relationship with her brother.

He was surprised to find that over the next hour he genuinely enjoyed himself. The atmosphere was relaxed with lots of amusing stories being shared, including some about Josh's childhood. Damian squirreled them all away for later. He stopped mid-laugh at something amusing Camilla had said as a hand landed on his thigh. Not Josh's hand. That would have been more than welcome. But a meaty paw that came from the opposite side. It squeezed gently, causing Damian to glance down at the tattooed knuckles. *What the fuck was he meant to do?*

Taking his frozen stupor as acceptance, the hand inched its way upward settling on his upper thigh. Damian swallowed with difficulty. He couldn't move any farther away without climbing into Josh's lap. There were no empty seats, so moving to another wasn't an option. He could excuse himself to the restroom, but then, who was to say that as soon as he sat back down again, Hawk wouldn't just continue pawing at him. The only other options meant causing a scene, which would definitely ruin the current party atmosphere.

Damian risked a glance at Hawk's face, hoping to catch his eye and communicate without words that the man needed to get his damn hands off him or else. But Hawk stared studiously ahead, even turning to smile at his girlfriend like a complete sleazebag. Damian might make porn, but his scene partners were all guys roughly his own age with an athletic build. The bulky biker type had never been his thing. He didn't find Hawk remotely attractive, and it wasn't as if he'd given him even the slightest bit of encouragement during their very short acquaintance.

Just as Damian reached boiling point and was about to say to hell with it and tell the man where to go, scene or no scene, the hand gave one last squeeze before moving back across to its own space. Damian let his breath escape in a rush, relieved beyond belief that he wasn't going to have to ruin the lunch. Hopefully, Hawk had gotten the message. He had to have noticed that Damian's rigid muscles beneath his palm were far from welcoming.

"Oh. My. God. I do not believe it!"

The loud announcement at the side of the table caused Damian to momentarily forget his dilemma. He lifted his head to find two young guys standing there staring at him and Josh with their mouths wide open. He would have put them around eighteen or nineteen. Definitely no older than twenty. One had blond hair which was shaved around the back but longer on top, while his friend was a redhead.

The blond was the first to regain the power of speech, although as soon as words started tumbling from his mouth, Damian would have given anything in the world for him to have stayed mute forever. "Angel and Leo in the same damn place. As soon as I found out that Angel was from Blackpool, I said to Corey that we just might see him here one day if we were lucky. Didn't I, Corey?" His redheaded companion nodded profusely. "And you didn't believe me, did you, Corey?" This time his friend shook his head. "But here he is. I am *such* a huge fan of yours, Angel. I can't tell you. That scene you did with Tyler was absolutely to die for. *So* sexy."

His gaze darted to Damian. "No offence, Leo. But you know, you're new. You haven't done as many as this guy. What you have done, has been great though, hasn't it, Corey?" Another enthusiastic nod. He fished in his pocket, pulling out his phone. "Do you think we could have a selfie together? All four of us. I know you're in the middle of dinner, but we're so stoked to bump into you. There's no way we couldn't come over and say something. Anyway, I'm sure you love having fans, right." He winked. "After all, we're the ones that pay the subscription fee every month just to see you naked."

Corey finally found his voice, letting out a loud giggle. "Naked."

Blondy elbowed him. "Shut up! I told you to play it cool. If I can manage it, then so can you." He turned his attention back to the table. "I can't get over the two of you being here together." His mouth opened in a gasp. "Are you two a thing, or have you been filming here this weekend? Tell me we're going to get some naked beach action. That would be so fucking cool if it was filmed in my hometown." He frowned. "It's a bit cold though, isn't it?"

Damian managed to get his neck to move enough to be able to scan the faces around the table. The expressions varied between shock and confusion, some of them seemingly having already worked out what was going on, while others were a bit slower on the uptake. As for Josh, he was so rigid that he might as well have been made from stone.

It was Emily who eventually broke the silence. "What's he talking about, Josh? Subscription fee. Filming. Naked. It makes it sound like you"—she let out a little nervous laugh—"make porn or something. Why aren't you saying anything?"

Blondy pointed across the table in Emily's direction. "Who's this?"

"My sister." Josh's voice came out as a strangled whisper. *Poor Josh*. Damian couldn't see any way that Josh could manage to dig himself out of the hole that had just been created for him by a pair of over-enthusiastic fans. Neither of them had factored that into their weekend machinations. "And that's my mum and my dad over there, just in case you're interested."

"Oh! I thought they worked for the studio." Blondy's lips formed a perfect "o" and then stayed like that, until he seemed to give himself a mental shake. Corey leaned forward and whispered something in his ear. "I think..." Blondy took a step back, narrowly avoiding walking into his friend. "...we might not have picked the best time to come and talk to you. So you know what, don't worry about the selfie. We can see you're busy. I love you though, Angel. You're the best. Love your..." His eyes flicked to Josh's mum, evidently deciding it would be better not to finish what he'd been going to say. Corey grabbed his arm and dragged him away from the table before he could say anything else.

A stunned silence descended, no one seeming to know quite where to look. Josh's mum coughed. "I think you might owe us some sort of explanation."

Josh exhaled loudly but didn't say anything. Damian wanted to help in some way, but what could he do? It was up to Josh whether he was going to tell the truth or come up with some sort of elaborate lie. He couldn't make that decision for him. All he could do was try and offer support. To that end, he reached out, grabbing Josh's hand and giving it a supportive squeeze.

"Yes, I make... porn." There was a collective murmur from the table, Josh waiting until it had subsided before continuing. "I have for three years. It pays well and I'm not ashamed of it. It's... enjoyable."

Damian was proud of Josh for being so matter of fact about it. Josh's family didn't look like they were sharing quite the same sentiments. Camilla appeared as if she'd rather be anywhere in the world while the rest of the family all wore small frowns. Only Hawk looked like he was completely unaffected. Almost like he'd already known about it. *Fuck!* That explained a lot. No wonder he'd thought Damian would be up for messing about with him. It was an assumption a lot of people made when they knew you made porn.

Shifting around in his seat, Josh's voice sounded almost pleading when he spoke. "Can someone say something, please."

It was Emily who obliged. "If you're not ashamed of it, then why haven't you told us about it? Three years is a long time to keep a secret like that, Josh. Did you think we'd be mad?"

Josh ran a hand through his hair. "I know and I'm sorry. I *was* going to tell you." His glance encompassed the whole table. "But it never seemed to be the right time and I guess, yeah, I was a bit scared what you'd think."

"Are you safe?"

Josh turned to his mum in response to her question, his voice softening. "Yes, of course I'm safe. I'm not stupid." He lowered his voice, although Damian suspected that everyone in the restaurant already had a pretty good idea what was going on, judging by the unnatural quiet from the occupied tables. "It's condoms only and they also test regularly."

Camilla leaned forward. She seemed to have gotten over her initial shock and now appeared as if she were fascinated by the whole thing. "And you film there as well, Damian? With Josh?"

Crap! He'd been hoping they'd leave him out of it. "Erm... yeah. Not for three years, though. Just for a couple of months."

Emily tipped her head to the side, looking thoughtful. She giggled. "So that's where you met? Love blossomed on the porn studio floor. How romantic. What happened? You were both reaching for the same condom and your hands met."

Josh sighed. "I should probably come completely clean." Damian closed his eyes. It was obvious where this was going and it wasn't going to cast either of them in a very good light. He didn't blame Josh. It was hard to confess to one secret while still harboring another. He steeled his heart in an attempt not to care. After all, it was unlikely he was ever going to see any of them again after the weekend's charade came to an end. But for some reason he did care. He liked them. They'd accepted him and been nothing but friendly, and now Josh was about to reveal his part in the ongoing weekend's deception. He grabbed Josh's sleeve, selfishness winning out. "Josh, maybe you shouldn't."

His hand was shaken off, Josh giving him a small apologetic smile. "Sorry, I have to."

He turned to his family. "You know how you always give me a hard time for turning up at family gatherings on my own when everyone else is in a pair?"

Emily frowned. "We're only teasing. It's what families do. We don't mean anything by it. You'd do the same to me."

"Well, I decided I'd had enough of it. And I have to say it's been lovely this weekend to get a break from it." Damian braced himself for what was coming. "So, yeah. Damian's not my boyfriend. We only met the other day. He was kind enough to offer to play the part this weekend. Whatever you do, don't blame him though. This is my fault, not his."

His gaze dropped to Damian's lap, his eyes widening. There'd been so much going on in the last ten minutes, so many big reveals that Damian hadn't even noticed that at some point Hawk's hand had reappeared on his thigh. It had to have been recent. What kind of sleazebag used family drama as an excuse to cop a feel? Josh's gaze whipped to Hawk's face. "How about you get your hand off my boyfriend before I chop it off."

Shrugging, Hawk pulled his hand back onto his own lap, not even bothering to look guilty. Josh's gaze found Damian's. "I'm sorry I didn't believe you before. I should have done."

Damian wished there was a magic switch he could press. One which would take him away from this table and back to London. Maybe where he could wake up in bed and discover it had all been a dream. It wouldn't be the first one he'd had about Angel. "It's fine."

"What did you think you were doing?"

Damian lifted his head to find Emily staring accusingly at her boyfriend. She seemed to be hovering somewhere between anger and upset, ready to come down on either side depending on what response she got.

Hawk crossed his arms, his massive biceps tensing. "You knew I was bisexual. I told you. And you agreed to an open relationship."

Mike began to choke on his drink, Camilla leaning over to hammer him on the back until he could breathe again. Josh's dad opened his mouth to speak and then closed it again without saying anything.

Tears spilled over, Emily rubbing at her eyes in an effort to stop them from flowing. "I can't believe you just said that in front of my parents. I knew we were having issues but I didn't know that meant you were going to start groping my brother's boyfriend in front of me. How could you? We agreed to discuss anyone that we were interested in."

Josh interjected. "It's not the first time either. He was playing footsie with him under the table yesterday as well." He offered an apologetic smile in Damian's direction. "Damian told me but I thought he was imagining it. I'm sorry, Em. I thought"—he shot a venomous glance in Hawk's direction—"he was okay. But apparently he isn't. He's the type of person that gets his kicks by groping other people's boyfriends."

Hawk leaned forward. "He's not your boyfriend. He's your pretend boyfriend."

Josh let out a huff. "You didn't know that though, did you? Not the first time you did it and not the second either."

Hawk turned his head sideward, his gaze roving over Damian's face before doing the same to his body. It made Damian want to scrub himself in the shower. "He's pretty."

"I think..." Everyone turned to look at Miranda as she spoke. She rubbed her temples as if to ward off the beginning of a headache. "...we've probably discussed this enough in a public place. I think we should get the bill and then go home and discuss this somewhere private."

There was a series of nods from around the table. Some birthday lunch this had turned out to be. Damian felt like crap and it wasn't even his family. He reluctantly put some space between himself and Josh. He could hardly keep himself plastered to his side now that everyone knew that they weren't a couple. He missed his warmth and scent immediately. The moment they went their separate ways in a few hours was going to be absolute hell. He was already dreading it.

Chapter Eight

JOSH WASN'T ENTIRELY sure whether it was a good thing or a bad thing that his mum's version of talking once they'd gotten back to the house was a one-on-one interrogation, rather than a group discussion. Given that he and Damian needed to be on the road within an hour for the return journey to London, Josh was the first to be summoned. For some reason, despite the fact that Emily clearly wasn't talking to him, Hawk had still returned with them to the house. He seemed to be under the misapprehension that Emily was going to look past his wandering hands and forgive him. Josh knew his sister though. After the initial tears, she was well on her way to being furious. Once she'd gotten the discussion with their mum out of the way, no doubt Hawk would be next. Hawk might think she was in the bathroom crying but Josh would have laid odds on her actually planning her dumping speech. It was a shame he wasn't going to be around to witness it, but then, there'd probably been enough drama for one day.

He glared at Hawk on the way to the front room, trying to communicate through his expression alone that he needed to keep his dirty hands off Damian in his absence. The big lug simply smirked at him. God only knows what Emily had ever seen in him. He offered a tight smile to Damian and then followed his mum to his doom.

She led him into the front room, closed the door firmly, and then stood with her hands on her hips and looked at him. He wilted under the intense stare, caving after less than ten seconds. "Get it over with, please."

"I'm disappointed in you, Joshua Andrew Keating."

He winced. Not only was she full-naming him, but the words themselves stung. He couldn't remember her ever expressing disappointment in him before. He opened his mouth to defend himself, but she held a hand up before he could speak. "And before you jump to conclusions, I'm not disappointed in you because you make adult films. As long as they're above board and everything is safe and you're not being corrupted by some sleazy producer, then you're an adult and you can do whatever you want. You know your father and I have always been very open with things like that. We've watched porn."

Josh couldn't help it. He covered his ears with his hands. He'd rather his parents disowned him than discussed their porn-watching habits with him. There were certain things he never wanted to think about when it came to his parents. Their sex life was one of them. "Please don't. I don't want to know."

His mum stepped forward, yanking on his wrist so that he was forced to take his hands away. "I'm disappointed in you because you lied. For years, Josh. That hurts. It really does. What made you feel like you couldn't tell us?"

"I don't know." He was being honest. He really didn't know. Especially in light of how cool his mum was being about the whole thing. And out of the two of them, his mum was the least easy-going. His dad would just go along with whatever she said. "It just seemed like something I should keep to myself.

And I wasn't lying back at the restaurant, I really did intend to tell you one day, but time passed and it just seemed to get harder and harder to do. I'm sorry."

"Are you going to keep doing it?"

"I think so. At least until I get my degree anyway. And then maybe even after that. This is probably not what you want to hear from your son, but I'm good at it."

His mum smiled, her eyes twinkling. "Of course you are. You've got a mixture of your father's and my genes. You apply yourself to whatever you do. Just promise me that you won't lie about it again."

Guilt gnawed at his bones. There was a slight sense of relief, though, now that it was finally out in the open. "I promise." Josh meant it as well. He pulled his mum in for a brief but heartfelt hug. He was lucky, really. She'd gone easy on him, rather than reading him the riot act. Oh, he was sure there'd be further discussions on the subject but it could definitely have been worse. Josh turned toward the door, eager to go and check that Hawk hadn't cornered Damian somewhere.

"Where are you going?"

Josh froze mid-step before turning slowly back to face her. "I thought we were done."

His mum tilted her head to one side, her eyebrow quirked. "That was item one on the agenda."

"It was?"

She crossed her arms and lifted her chin. "Oh, definitely. Now we need to talk about that poor, sweet boy you conned into helping you lie."

"Poor, sweet boy? Oh, you mean Damian." He stifled a laugh at the rather bizarre description that didn't seem to fit him at all. He might blush, but he was far from sweet and innocent. He'd proved that last night.

"How did you manage to talk him into getting involved in your devious plan to pull the wool over our eyes?"

"It wasn't like that." Thinking back, if anything it had been the other way around. *Strange, really.* "He was happy to come. I think he just wanted a weekend away."

"He's a sweet boy."

Josh's lips curled of their own volition. "He is."

"You could do a lot worse than to have someone like him for a boyfriend. A real boyfriend, I mean. Not a fake one."

"I could. But..." He had no idea where he was going with that sentence so he just left it hanging.

"Don't think we didn't hear you last night. Your fake relationship didn't seem to stop you from having fun." She raised an eyebrow. "Noisy fun."

Had they been that loud? He'd been telling the truth when he'd told Damian they'd be asleep. "Sorry."

"I hope you didn't take advantage of him?"

"I didn't. I promise." Seduced him into letting his barriers down, maybe. But he hadn't taken advantage of him. Damian had been only too willing once he'd worked out what was going on. The thought made him want to take Damian upstairs and do it all over again.

"You must have noticed that he likes you. He's been all over you all weekend. It was *very* convincing. *Too* convincing."

It was obvious what she was implying, the idea making his palms go clammy. That didn't necessarily make it true, though. "He's a drama student. He's just a good actor." Only, there'd been no reason for him to act when they were on their own.

When they were at the Pleasure Beach, or kissing on the beach. Or when there'd just been the two of them in the bedroom. So that explanation only went so far.

His mum walked over to the door, pulling it open. "Maybe. Just saying that perhaps during your long drive home, you should talk to him."

He smiled at her before leaning over and kissing her on the cheek. "I think perhaps you're right." His mouth went dry at the thought.

"I usually am." She sighed wearily. "Right. Now, I need to talk to your sister about how long this 'open relationship' thing has been going on and make sure she's going to give Hawk his marching orders. After all the other reveals, I half expected your brother to tell me that he's become a drag queen on the weekends."

A bubble of laughter escaped from Josh's throat. "I don't think there's any danger of that. He'd look terrible in a dress and he can't even paint a wall, never mind put make-up on."

DAMIAN'S GAZE MADE Josh's skin tingle as he joined him at the car. He'd tried to make the goodbyes a little less awkward for Damian by suggesting that he take the bags out and wait for him there. He'd jumped at the opportunity and who could blame him. They both climbed in and closed the doors. When Josh still didn't say anything, Damian finally ran out of patience. "Was it awful?"

Josh fastened his seatbelt before offering any response. "Actually no, it wasn't. It should have been." He risked a glance across to his fake ex-boyfriend. God, he was cute. He seemed to have grown exponentially more attractive with every hour that had passed that weekend. Having sex with him had only compounded that further. He gave himself a mental shake. "My mum was more understanding than she should have been about the fact that I've been lying to her for three years. I wouldn't say she's *happy* about the fact that I make porn. But she wasn't as shocked as I thought she might be. I wish I'd told her years ago. I *should* have told her years ago."

Damian smiled. "That's good. And what about..." He waved a hand between the two of them to signify what he was talking about.

Well, that was an interesting question, wasn't it? Josh was still struggling to wrap his head around the insights his mum had put forward on that subject. He wasn't about to share those thoughts with Damian, though. Not yet, anyway. He busied himself with inserting the key into the ignition and starting the engine.

"Well?"

Damian obviously wasn't prepared to go without an answer. Josh pulled out into traffic. "She liked you. They all did." That's all he was prepared to give him at the moment.

"Hawk liked me."

Josh snorted. It was good that Damian could joke about it. Especially after Josh had been such a dick by not believing him. He cast a quick glance over at Damian, noting the blush was back. "Well, I suspect that he's going to be free and single soon. So just let me know if you need me to put a good word in for you."

The sound Damian produced was similar to one he imagined a cat might make if it was being slowly suffocated. "No, thank you. He's not my type."

"What is your type?" Josh's fingers tightened around the steering wheel. But apart from that, he was proud of how nonchalant he managed to sound. Like it was just a polite enquiry to pass the time. He and Damian might have fucked but that didn't mean anything apart from that Josh had been the best thing on offer at the time. Besides, he'd virtually had to sweet-talk him out of the sweatpants.

There was a long pause while Damian considered his response. *Was he thinking about it? Or trying to work out how he could avoid answering altogether?* Feeling bad, Josh cut in. "Sorry. None of my business. Just trying to make conversation, considering we've got a long journey back to London. We can talk about something else if you'd rather? Something less personal."

The seat squeaked as Damian shifted. "No, it's fine. I was just... thinking. I don't mind answering. Sounds like a cliché but tall, dark, and muscular. That's about it, really."

The description fit Josh perfectly. He tried reasoning with the glow of satisfaction that immediately flared to life, telling it that it would also fit millions more men in the population, but it persisted anyway.

"Why are you smiling?"

Fuck! Had he been? It was easy to forget that while Josh's gaze was focused on the road in front of them, Damian's was free to roam wherever it wished. Including on him. "Was I? Oh, I just thought it was funny that your description was so vague."

Damian let out a huff, but at least he didn't call Josh a liar. "What about you? What's your type?"

Rapidly changing. "Angel doesn't have a type. He's happy with whatever he can get."

"I'm not asking about Angel." The frown in Damian's voice was all too obvious even without being able to see his facial expression. "What's Josh's type?"

"Josh is..." He stopped himself before he could launch into talking about himself in the third person, as if Angel was more real than Josh was. One of the many benefits of Angel was that Josh could pull him out at will as a nice little diversion. Apparently, that wasn't going to wash with Damian. "I'm fussy." That was the truth. He was. He'd only had three boyfriends in the past year and all of the relationships had been fairly short-lived.

One had wanted him to give up porn, one hadn't managed to square it in his mind that Josh wanted to get fucked, instead of fucking, and the third had seemed far more interested in his motorbike than he was in Josh. The problem was that a porn career meant that he didn't need a relationship to get sex. Okay, it was sex of a slightly different kind with people watching and angles carefully rehearsed. But at the end of the day, it still ended in an orgasm. Therefore, any possible boyfriend prospects needed to offer a lot more. He mulled over what that was as he pulled up at a red light. Friendship. *Like Damian.* Good conversation. *Like Damian.* Fun. *Like Damian.* Yeah, it was official, Damian ticked all of the boxes.

Now, he just needed to find a way of discovering whether Damian might be interested in turning their fake relationship into something more real. Just like his mum had suggested. Not here, though. Not where he could only spare the odd glance in

Damian's direction. He wanted to be able to see his face properly. "Do you want to stop somewhere on the way back? Grab a coffee? Maybe a snack? It'll split the journey up."

"Sure. Sounds good."

Chapter Nine

FOR THE FIRST TIME that weekend, conversation seemed to have fizzled out between the two of them. Damian had tried broaching a couple of subjects, but Josh seemed lost in his own head. There was definitely something weird going on with him. It would have been easy to put it down to everything that had happened over lunch. After all, who wouldn't struggle with their porn career, their fake relationship, their sister's open relationship, and her boyfriend's propensity for groping unwilling victims all being uncovered in the space of ten minutes. That had to mess with anybody's head. It was messing with his. And it wasn't even his family.

Except Josh had seemed fine when he'd first gotten in the car. Relaxed, even. It could be some sort of delayed reaction, but it didn't seem likely. No, whatever was bothering him was something else. Had he worked out that Damian hadn't exactly been straight with him? *How though?* Had Damian said something that had given him away? If so, he couldn't recall anything. He'd done a pretty good job at answering the question about his type without giving too much away, managing to hold back from adding any extra details like tanned with dimples. No doubt then Josh would have realized that the description fitted him to a T.

The more miles they traveled down the motorway, and the longer the silence stretched between them, the more Damian needed to come clean, the guilt riding him like a demon on his back. Chances were that he wasn't going to see Josh again after this weekend. Not in a personal capacity, anyway. He might bump into him as Angel, but even that seemed unlikely given how long it had taken for their paths to cross in the first place.

Thinking about Josh as Angel, reminded him of something else that still bothered him. The honesty reveal could wait until they'd made their stop, but this was something Damian could clear up now. He just needed to be careful how he phrased it, make sure it was casual enough so that the answer—whatever it might be—came across as not bothering him one little bit. "Why did you refuse to film a scene with me?" Damian could have kicked himself. He couldn't have sounded less casual if he'd ended the query with a sob.

Josh's gaze flicked from the road to him, his brow creasing into a frown. "What do you mean, refuse?"

Damian swallowed. He'd started the conversation. There was no backing out of it now. Not without making himself look like an even bigger idiot than he had already. "I asked Evan if I could film a scene with you and he told me you'd said no. I'm just curious, why?" He squeezed his lips together before they could manage to betray him and ask what was wrong with him. Something shriveled in Damian's chest as Josh laughed. Not just a little laugh, but a full-bellied one as if Damian had said something hilarious. If they hadn't been travelling at seventy miles per hour down a busy motorway, Damian would have been tempted to jump out of the moving vehicle.

There was another glance thrown his way from Josh, who'd finally stopped laughing. "You seriously think I get any say whatsoever who I film with?"

The tight feeling in Damian's chest eased slightly. "You don't? But Evan said..."

Josh's fingers tightened around the steering wheel and Damian had to drag his mind away from the memory of those hands on his body. Josh offered a quick smile. "Listen, Evan's a great guy. He really is. But he's first and foremost a businessman. He loves his models to believe that the studio's a democracy, but it really isn't. He calls all the shots and is quite happy to twist the truth a little to make himself look like the innocent party. I reckon he's got a noticeboard at home with all the pairings planned for the next year. He likes to make it look casual, but it isn't. I assure you that your request never got as far as me. And I've never turned anyone down. Why would I? It doesn't matter to me who I film with. Josh is fussy. Angel isn't."

Damian had been feeling a lot better until Josh's last comment. "Nobody? There must be someone you wouldn't want to film with?"

Josh shook his head. "No, it's work. A performance. I don't have to like a guy to pretend I like him." He gestured out of the window at the approaching turn-off. "Let's go to these services. I could do with stretching my legs for a bit, and a shot of caffeine would also be good."

***

JOSH HAD RETURNED TO brooding, which would be okay if it didn't make him seem even sexier. Damian found himself watching him as Josh stared into his coffee, the last few remnants of his croissant on a plate in front of him. Finally, Josh lifted his head, staring at Damian intently for a few seconds before speaking. "I wanted to tell you something. Well, ask you something, really."

Damian interrupted him, the small fire of guilt, having grown to a huge, great furnace. If he didn't get it out now, he never would. "I need to confess something first. Something I might not have been completely honest about."

Josh's expression was curious as he reached out, picking up a piece of croissant and crumbling it between his fingers. "Go on."

When one deep breath didn't seem adequate, Damian allowed himself another. It was difficult to know where to start, but he decided to go with the lesser of the lies he'd told first. At least in his head it was. "I'm not a drama student."

The only expression on Josh's face was a tiny lift of one eyebrow—no discomfort. So far, so good. Damian decided he should probably elaborate. "I'm a music student. So, it's still the arts. Just... not the one I said."

"Why would you lie about that?"

That was an excellent question. Why had he lied? He cast his mind back, but the beginning of the weekend felt like it had been months ago, rather than forty-eight hours. In fact, less than that. "I think I wanted to convince you that I'd be good. You know, so you wouldn't be too worried about me being able to play the part of your boyfriend convincingly."

Josh sat back in his chair, his gaze fixed on Damian's face as if he were trying to see through his skin to what lay beneath. "You were. Very convincing, that is. Which is surprising if you're not an actor."

"Yeah, about that. It was convincing because..." Damian would have given anything to have a croissant to crumble the same way that Josh was doing, but unfortunately, he'd eaten all of his. He gripped on to the side of the table instead. *Was he really going to do this?* His heart was going a hundred miles an hour, the mere idea of putting his crush into words giving him palpitations. Maybe he shouldn't say anything? Only, Josh was staring at him and waiting for him to speak, so he had to say something. And his mind was blank of anything but the truth.

He dipped his head, finding it easier to focus on the table rather than Josh's face, his gaze tracing a line of crumbs that had escaped Josh's plate. "...because, I kind of already had a thing for you. Well, not you, Angel, I guess, because I didn't really know you. That's why I was so keen to volunteer for this weekend so I could spend time with you." When his announcement was met with nothing but silence, Damian steeled himself before lifting his head.

Josh was staring at him like he wasn't sure what to make of him. "So, you're saying what? You saw me at the studio and gained a bit of a thing for me?"

Damian winced. "Not quite."

"What does that mean?"

"I kind of joined the studio because I wanted to meet you. I'd watched all of your videos before that. I was... I am a huge fan." There it was, the absolute truth was out there. Damian felt like he'd just scraped his innards out and left them on display. "I figured this weekend would be a chance to get to know you. The real you. And it was fun, wasn't it? Apart from the last bit where everything came crashing down. And last night was..." He paused at the pained expression on Josh's face at the reminder of what they'd done. "I'm not a stalker." Okay, saying that made it sound like he was. He needed some way to dig himself out of the deep hole he'd made for himself.

But Josh had already drained the last of his coffee and stood. "We should probably get back to London. We've both got lectures tomorrow."

That was it? He wasn't going to say anything else? Damian would have preferred him to get mad, or call him names, or do something. Anything would have been preferable to nothing. "Josh?"

"Do you need the restroom or anything?"

Damian shook his head and followed Josh back to the car. They were only about an hour away from London. It was probably going to be the longest hour of his life.

APART FROM THE CONVERSATION needed to establish where Damian wanted to be dropped off, Josh had barely said two words during the last part of the journey. At least Damian hadn't been left at the services. God knows how he would have gotten back to London if that had happened. He glanced over as the car drew to a halt outside his apartment building. Was it worth a last-gasp attempt to try and get them back on an even keel? But Josh was just staring straight ahead, his knuckles white as he gripped the steering wheel, even though the car was now stationary.

Damian sighed. There was only so long the two of them could sit there in silence outside his apartment block until it got to whatever came after excruciatingly awkward. If only he'd kept his fucking mouth shut. It seemed like honesty really wasn't the best policy. He twisted around, dragging his bag from the back seat into the front between the gap in the two seats. "Well, I guess I better go." With a heavy heart, and already planning a descent into comfort food, he reached for the door handle.

"Wait!"

Damian froze. He slowly unfurled his fingers from the handle and twisted back around to face Josh. The pained expression was back on his face. It was obvious he wanted to say something but wasn't quite at the point of being able to say it. Damian placed his bag in the footwell, hoping the action was enough to demonstrate that he was happy to wait, no matter how long it took. Josh swallowed, his tanned throat contracting. Damian did his best not to look at him like he wanted to lick him all over but it took just about all the restraint he had.

"So you had a thing for Angel? Since when?"

"I don't know. I can't put an exact date on it. You hadn't been at the studio that long, I don't think. I seem to remember you having about six or seven videos on the site at the time."

"And you watched them all?"

It was a bit too late for Josh to get hung up on that fact, considering that less than twenty-four hours ago, he'd been only too happy to watch one *with* Damian. "Yes. Several times."

"I see."

What did that mean? "I've seen all your videos." *Shut up, you idiot. Stop making things worse.*

"And you joined the studio because you wanted to meet me? And then you asked Evan if you could film a scene? And when he said no, you invited yourself along to my parents' house for the weekend?"

Damian's brow furrowed. "Hang on! You're making this sound far worse than it is. You needed someone to help you and I offered because I wanted you to notice me. That's all. I wasn't the one who instigated sex. You did."

A muscle ticked in Josh's cheek. "I definitely noticed you."

Damian rubbed his palm over his left eye, trying to work out where this conversation was going and what the last cryptic comment was supposed to mean. Was Josh just trying to make him feel bad or was there some other purpose to it? His hand twitched closer to his bag. Maybe it would be better to cut his losses and get out of the car? At least then he could lick his wounds in private.

Josh stared into space. "I'm struggling to get my head around everything you've told me."

"I'm sorry." There wasn't a lot else that Damian could say.

"Angel and I are very different people." Blue eyes swung in his direction. "You wanted a weekend with Angel, right?"

Damian frowned. Surely, Josh didn't think that he'd prefer a fantasy over the real thing? Yes, this had all come from his initial fixation on Angel, but it had grown to so much more over the weekend. He picked his words carefully, sensing it was something of a sore point with Josh. "I liked Angel because he was the only aspect of you that I ever got to see. And he was sexy and cool and completely out of reach. Then I got to spend the weekend with Josh. With you. The real you. At least I hope you were being completely genuine, and I learned..." He paused, unable to hold back a smile. "...I liked Josh even more. I actually got a chance to get to know you. And I gotta tell you, that was a hundred times better than watching you get it on with other guys. And yes, maybe I took advantage of the situation slightly. But you were right there and I had permission to touch you. So I did. If it makes you feel better, I doubt I'll watch your videos anymore."

"Why not?"

Okay. Now he sounded upset that Damian wasn't going to watch them. Josh needed to make his damn mind up. Damian let out an exasperated sigh. "Because it'll be a painful reminder of the one night that we got to spend together." He turned away, his fingers wrapping around the handle of his bag and yanking it onto his knee. Damian needed to get out of there. "Happy now?" He reached for the door, only to hear the click as the central locking was engaged. He refused to turn around. "Let me out!"

"Damian."

He tugged on the handle harder even though he knew it was a pointless exercise. Damian flinched as a hand landed on his shoulder, gently turning him around until he reluctantly faced Josh. Josh smiled but it was a cautious one. "You like me, then?"

He shrugged the hand off, the touch causing the rebellious part of his brain to want to strip all his clothes off and spread himself out naked for Josh. "Yes, I like you. I've liked you for years and now I like you even more."

The smile on Josh's face grew even wider. "Do you remember I wanted to talk to you about something back at the services? Just before you decided to drop your truth bomb on me."

He had. He remembered now. Only Damian had been too worried that if he waited any longer to say what he needed to, he might have chickened out altogether so he'd interrupted. "What were you going to say?"

Josh's expression turned decidedly sheepish. "I was going to ask if you were at all interested in making this fake thing real. In fact, that is what I'm asking. Just so there's no misunderstandings between us. How about it?" The words might have been delivered casually, but the way his fingers curled reflexively into his thigh were anything but. Josh was nervous? Because of him?

Breathing had always seemed to come so easily to Damian before. Only now, it seemed like the most difficult thing in the world to do as he ran the words over and over in his brain, trying to make sure that he wasn't jumping to the wrong conclusion. No matter which way he rearranged them, they always came out the same way. Josh flipping Keating was interested in him. Not just in a "you're in the same bed, we as may well fuck" way, but in a more permanent way. Damian's heart raced, his face feeling like every bit of the blood in his body had suddenly rushed there. "You're asking me to be your boyfriend? Your real boyfriend?"

Josh's lips quirked, revealing a tantalizing hint of dimple. "I'm suggesting that we continue where we left off this weekend and get to know each other better. Then see where it goes from there."

"Yes!" The word left Damian's mouth without going through his brain first. Not that he would have said anything different, had he spent an extra two seconds considering it.

"Want to think about it for a bit longer?"

Even Josh's teasing couldn't dampen the rush of elation. Besides, there was no reason to play it cool when he'd already admitted to panting after Josh for years, even if it was in the guise of Angel. "No."

There was a click of a seatbelt releasing and then Josh was right there, leaning in, his lips on Damian's. Damian closed his eyes and melted into it, his hand coming up to cup Josh's cheek. They may have kissed before, but this felt like the first one. In a way it was—the first real one anyway, without any sort of charade, pretense, or secrets between them. Damian parted his lips, eagerly accepting Josh's tongue when it was offered and meeting it with his own. The kiss started slow, but gradually picked up speed and heat, until they were both breathless and laughing when they finally broke apart.

Damian pointed toward the building they'd been parked outside for the last ten minutes, the throbbing of his crotch demanding that he ask the question that was on the tip of his tongue. "Want to come up?"

Josh peered past him as if his decision was dependent on a careful scrutiny of the brickwork. "You don't think we should take it slowly?"

A laugh escaped from Damian's throat before he could stop it. "You don't think that ship has well and truly sailed, given that we had sex last night? Twice. Oh, and then there's the fact that we both make porn so we're not exactly hung up on sharing our bodies."

Josh's lips twitched. "Good point." He dropped another quick kiss on Damian's lips. "In that case, lead the way."

Chapter Ten

JOSH HAD SURPRISED himself with how little it bothered him that Damian had been carrying a torch for him long before this weekend. Okay, that was simplifying it. It had bothered him at first. He'd spent the rest of the journey back to London after they'd left the services trying to weigh things up and work out how he felt about it, but a lot of that had been down to a niggle that it could have been Angel and not Josh that Damian wanted. He wasn't worried about Damian being a stalker. Stalkers didn't blush. Actually, the blush kind of made sense now. It was what you did around the guy you had a crush on. His mum had hit the nail on the head really, hadn't she? When she'd pointed out that Josh seemed as if he genuinely liked him. Ten out of ten for female intuition there. He wondered how much she'd gloat when he told her just how right she'd been.

He followed Damian into his apartment, barely resisting the urge to push him against the wall there and then. "Do you have roommates?"

Damian placed his bag down; Josh had left his in the car, but brought his laptop, phone, and wallet up, just in case. He placed them on a nearby table. Damian turned to smile at him. "One."

Good job he hadn't jumped on him, then. Or they'd be doing a live porn show right in the middle of the living room.

Damian winked. "She's away until next weekend."

Josh stalked forward, pressing Damian back against the arm of the sofa until their bodies were forced together, curls of sensation unfurling throughout his nervous system. "It took you far too long to say that."

"I thought you wanted to take things slow."

He fastened his hands on the waistband of Damian's sweatshirt, tugging upward until Damian cooperated and lifted his arms. He yanked it over his head, pleased when the T-shirt came with it, leaving Damian deliciously bare-chested. "You talked me out of it."

Damian seemed only too eager to reciprocate, quickly stripping Josh's top off, his fingers straying downward to trace his abdominal muscles. "I don't remember the 'talking you out of it' bit. I remember pointing out a couple of things and you agreeing straightaway. Within seconds. Not even that, really. Hundredths of a second."

Josh dropped his hands to the button on Damian's jeans, unfastening it before doing the same to his zipper. Damian obediently toed his shoes off before stepping out of his jeans. Josh raised an eyebrow, laughing, as Damian took the hint and shed his underwear as well. "Tom-ah-to. Tom-ay-to." He busied himself with shedding his own clothes until they were both equally naked.

Not touching any of the bare skin he'd uncovered was proving to be sweet torture for Josh, but the anticipation sizzling along his veins would make it all the more worthwhile in the end. He'd kind of hedged the boyfriend question in the car, crumbs of doubt still lurking in his brain. But right here, there was no question. If he already felt this way about Damian after less than forty-eight hours in his company—this mixture of lust, affection, and need—then there was no point in fighting it. No point at all.

"Come here, boyfriend."

Damian almost knocked him over, he shot across the space between them so fast, his body slamming into Josh's. Somehow, Josh managed to hold them both steady. He slid his hands around Damian's waist, unable to resist dropping them to the swell of his ass, his fingers exploring the taut, muscled skin. Damian smiled against Josh's shoulder. "Am I? What perks does that entail?"

Josh slid his hands even lower, pulling their groins more tightly together. "Erm... getting to spend time with me. Dates. Sex. Lots of sex. What else?"

He stopped talking when Damian laid a finger over his lips. "Stop right there. That's more than enough. You had me at getting to spend time with you."

Smiling, Josh made a mock attempt to bite Damian's finger. "Correct answer. Although, you say that now. What if the novelty quickly wears off?"

It was a relief when Damian actually gave the question serious consideration. "Well, that could work both ways. There's still an awful lot to learn about each other. We may have crammed to memorize the major details, but that's not really knowing each other. But..." Damian squirmed closer, rubbing his cock against Josh's stomach. "That can wait, right? Till tomorrow."

Damn, right. It could wait. Josh grabbed Damian's shoulders and spun him around, pinning him against the back of the sofa and crushing his body against his, his dick fitting perfectly into the notch of his butt cheeks. He leaned forward, plastering his front to Damian's back while he licked a line along his neck. "It can definitely wait. Can I fuck you?"

The sexy body in his arms went still. "I thought you didn't like topping in your personal life?"

Josh nuzzled closer, wrapping his arms around Damian's chest, and rubbing his stubble against the area on his neck he'd just tasted. "Let's just say that I like to bottom nine times out of ten and this is the tenth time."

Damian's chest shook as he laughed. "Wow! I must be suffering from severe memory loss. I remember us fucking twice, but I seem to have forgotten the other seven. Was I asleep?"

Shifting his hips slightly, Josh managed to find the perfect angle to rub his cock over Damian's hole, a little promise of what was to come if he said yes. That made two of them that was surprised that he was so keen to top Damian. But then, Damian did have a delectable ass: firm and muscled and oh so fuckable. Maybe with him it would become two times out of ten, or even three. "You don't want me to?"

It was a rhetorical question. The answer was already implicit in the way Damian was bending his body to help with the friction. The way he was arching his back to make it easier for Josh to do exactly what he wanted to do. It was also in the way his breathing had sped up, the heartbeat under his palm frantic. It was just a question of how much Damian was going to tease. How long they were going to play this game for it to ramp up the anticipation even more. As it turned out, the answer was not very long at all.

Damian let out a shuddering breath. "God! Yes, please. I need you inside me. I need to know what it feels like to get fucked by that magnificent cock."

He chuckled into the nape of Damian's neck. "Magnificent, eh? I'll definitely take that as a compliment." Josh, reluctantly, peeled himself away, taking a moment to step back and just stare at the long line of Damian's muscled back. They needed condoms. Only problem was they'd already used the two he'd had in his wallet the previous night. "Condoms. I don't have any."

Damian shifted restlessly. "In my bedroom down the hall. The one painted blue. Chest of drawers by the window. Top drawer." It would have probably made a lot more sense for Damian to go and get them himself, but Josh's cock wasn't really interested in sense. "Stay there. Don't move." He took a couple of steps backward, still unwilling to take his eyes off Damian in case this whole weekend was some sort of beautiful mirage that his brain had conjured up.

Damian turned his head to look back over his shoulder, his eyes finding Josh's. He shifted his position, bending farther forwards, his arms braced against the back of the sofa while his stance widened, his thighs bracing farther apart to display himself without any sign of inhibitions. Josh's cock throbbed insistently, the desire to bury himself between those muscular cheeks almost overwhelming. He needed to watch the rest of Damian's scenes as Leo. If he performed anything like this for the camera, then they must be scorching. A tiny part of Josh hoped that this was a special performance. One just for him.

"Are you just going to stare at me?"

The words snapped Josh out of his stupor, making him realize that was exactly what he'd been doing. He spun around, heading out of the door. Where had Damian said his room was? He flung a door open. Bathroom. No, that wasn't it. The next door was a bedroom, its walls painted cream. Damian had said blue. He kept going, finally finding a room painted blue. Yeah, it would definitely have made more sense for Damian to do this while Josh waited. The room looked like someone had left it in a hurry, clothes strewn everywhere as if Damian had packed for the weekend in a rush. Feeling a bit like a voyeur, Josh hastened over to the chest of drawers and pulled the top one open. Luckily, the condoms—and lube—were easy enough to locate. Grabbing them, he paused for a moment, counting to five in an effort to calm himself down.

He got as far as three before his cock completely took over his brain, pushing him back down the hallway and into the living room. Damian hadn't moved an inch, his hips pushed up invitingly. One thing was for sure, there wasn't going to be any foreplay this time. They had all night for that, though. He'd make it up to him later. Suck Damian's cock until he had him squirming and begging to come. Maybe rim the ass that he'd already fucked?

Josh stopped halfway across the room, watching the slight sway of Damian's ass, and loving the way his muscles bunched and relaxed whenever he shifted position slightly. "How do you like it?"

There was a pause while Damian considered the question. "Surprise me."

That meant that Damian was up for anything. Slow. Fast. Hard. Deep. His favorite type of bottom: one that just went with the flow, taking everything their partner had to give. Josh smiled as he smoothed a condom over his dick before adding a generous amount of lube and making sure that he had some on his fingers as well.

"Are you coming over here any time soon?" Damian's hips moved and Josh knew that he was rubbing his aching cock against the back of his sofa, searching for any stimulation he could find.

"Maybe."

Damian let out a groan. "You're killing me!"

He was killing himself, but he also needed to savor the moment of having his brand-new boyfriend stretched out in front of him, desperate for his cock. It might be the first time of many—at least he hoped so, but it was still a memorable moment. "You're so fucking hot."

"Then get over here. Please." The last word was stretched out into more of a moan than anything else. Damian sounded like he was going to cry if Josh made him wait any longer.

Josh made short work of the space between them, wasting no time in using his lubed fingers to probe between Damian's ass cheeks. He traced his rim before slowly easing one finger inside, Damian letting out an enthusiastic string of "Yeses," in response.

It didn't take long for Josh to locate his prostate. One of the perks of the job. If there were certificates for being able to find a prostate in record time, Angel would probably have a wall full of them. He rubbed his finger over it, using the palm of his other hand to hold Damian's back flat as he attempted to arch up. "You like that?"

"Mmmmphfff."

Josh introduced another finger, delighting in Damian's responses, the way he squirmed, the muffled noises and curses that kept spilling from his mouth. The way the tight channel wrapped around his fingers reflexively tightened and relaxed.

This just might be Josh's new favorite thing. "Your prostate's so sensitive. I reckon I could make you come just like this."

Damian let out a strangled laugh. "Tell me something I don't know. And yes, you could. I'm already so damn close." He arched up onto his tiptoes as Josh rubbed harder, only the hand on his back stopping him from trying to stand in an effort to alleviate the sweet torture on his prostate. "If I don't get your cock soon, I'm going to kill you."

Sliding his hand between Damian's body and the sofa, Josh found what he was looking for, his palm filling with Damian's stiff dick, the glans sticky with pre-cum. He gave it a couple of strokes, his fingers still rubbing that magic spot deep in Damian's ass. It was so tempting to just push him over the edge that way and feel him come apart on his fingers, his body quivering and shaking with the force of his orgasm. The only thing stopping him was the fact that it would feel even better on his cock. He forced himself to stop, leaning against Damian's sweaty back for a moment while he regained his composure. He reluctantly withdrew his fingers, laughing as Damian protested feebly. "If you want my cock, the fingers have to go. Unless you want both of them?"

"Not today."

Well, that was an interesting answer. It seemed like Damian was a bit of a size queen. He mentally readjusted his estimate of topping three times out of ten to four. Then his brain switched off entirely as he eased his cock into the space where his fingers had just been. They both let out a groan in unison. He felt so damn good. So tight. He wrenched Damian's head around, their lips meeting in a scorching kiss, Josh's tongue offering a promise of what his lower body would do once he was sure Damian's body had fully adjusted to his length.

It was Damian who broke first, his body pushing back against Josh's so insistently that he had no other option than to start thrusting, each slide of his cock up Damian's ass feeling like a slice of perfection. He straightened, bracing both of his hands on Damian's back as he gave him what he was crying out for, what both of them were crying out for. There was already a telltale tingle in Josh's balls that announced that his orgasm wasn't too far over the horizon. From the little gasps Damian was making, he was in the same boat.

Pulling Damian upright, Josh peeled him away from the sofa and wrapped his arms around Damian's chest to plaster them together, managing it without breaking the rhythm. Stupid as it was, he had to know something. He bit down on Damian's shoulder, his tongue laving the mark he'd left. "Say my name. Tell me how this is making you feel."

"It's so good. So good, Josh. Please don't stop. Yeah, just like that. Oh God, Josh."

Josh. Not Angel. Josh. He'd just needed that last bit of confirmation that Damian was after the real man, not the fantasy. He slid his hand down over Damian's abdomen, wrapping his fingers tightly around his cock and sliding his hand from root to tip. It only took a few strokes for Damian to jerk in his arms, his shout loud as hot cum spilled over Josh's fingers. Damian's reaction was enough to trigger Josh's own orgasm. He managed one more thrust, his teeth closing on Damian's shoulder again as a white-hot burst of pleasure flooded his body. For the next few seconds there was only sensation: the touch of skin, the tiny twitches of his still embedded cock, the combined sound of their rapid breaths, the twin thudding heartbeats.

It was Damian who recovered first, his fingers reaching up to tangle with Josh's where they still rested on his chest. "I need to sit down."

Josh laughed. That was an understatement if ever he'd heard one. He wasn't usually one for taking a nap after sex, but right now, it didn't seem like such a bad idea. He pulled back enough to separate their bodies, tugging Damian around to the opposite side of the sofa as he dropped the condom in the bin. He waited until Damian had made himself comfortable on the sofa before stretching out next to him. It was a tight fit, only made possible by lying half on top of him. But Josh was fine with that. More than fine. He wanted that closeness, that intimacy. He wrapped his hand around the back of Damian's neck, tugging him closer so that they could share a lazy kiss, both of them smiling as they broke apart.

Damian craned his neck so that he could look down at himself, his fingers probing his shoulder. "You bite!"

Josh leaned over to inspect the red mark. It was hard to feel apologetic when he liked seeing his mark on Damian's skin. Besides, from the expression on his lover's face, most of the outrage was very much staged. He settled for dropping a soft kiss on the reddened skin instead. When Damian squirmed, he went to town on it with lips and tongue until Damian was laughing, his cock already stirring against Josh's thigh. He reached down, rolling Damian's balls around in his palm before sliding his fingertips along the length of his cock "How long do you reckon before this little fella will be up for fucking me?"

Damian arched a brow. "Less of the little, thank you." He parted his thighs to give better access. There was no way Josh was turning down that invitation, his finger teasing the rim of Damian's lubed asshole. "About ten minutes if you keep that up."

Smiling, Josh let his finger sink deeper. "Yeah? I have no issue with that. No issue at all."

Epilogue

SIX MONTHS LATER

Damian sighed as he hung up the phone. It wasn't the first time that Evan had rung him asking if he could come in and film. But it was the shortest notice he'd ever been given. Normally, it was the next day, not how quickly can you get here? He hadn't even mentioned who Damian would be filming with. Yet Damian had felt obligated to say yes. He had no idea why really, apart from the fact that he wasn't doing anything else that afternoon and the extra money would come in handy. There was probably a bit of guilt mixed in there as well, considering he'd hardly filmed at all for them recently. His mind had been on other things. His lips curved into an automatic smile as he thought about one of those things in particular. A certain muscular boyfriend of his, who gave him more than enough orgasms.

It took him twenty minutes to get to the studio, no one responding to his calls of "hello," once he'd arrived. Given he was a last-minute stand-in, they were probably already in place to film. He took a quick shower without getting his hair wet before putting his underwear back on and making his way to the room where they usually filmed. Sure enough, quiet conversation drifted down the corridor, too quiet to identify exactly who was in there, but audible enough to show that the room was occupied.

Damian pushed the door open and walked in. Adam, the cameraman, was lounging over on the far side of the room, examining his fingernails, obviously waiting to start. Evan was straddling a chair backwards, his muscular arms draped over its back as he chatted to the man on the bed. The man who was incredibly familiar to Damian, given that they'd been together now for the past six months. Only they'd decided not to share that information with anyone at the studio, Evan included. Plenty of the guys had boyfriends. The only difference with Josh and Damian was that they both happened to work there.

All three pairs of eyes turned Damian's way as he entered the room. Adam offered a curt nod while Evan clapped his hands together. "There he is! Told you I'd found a replacement." Damian couldn't have said what Josh's reaction was because he couldn't bring himself to even glance in that direction. They'd agreed early in their relationship that they'd never film a scene together, so the only explanation for them being in the same room was that neither of them had known about it. Evan gestured to the bed. "Usual start position, Leo, please." He always called them by their studio names whenever they were ready to start filming, claiming it made it easier to avoid slipping up once the cameras were rolling.

Damian edged his way toward the bed, keeping his gaze focused on the sheets and refusing to let his eyes drift upward. *Was Josh going to say something?* When there was nothing but silence, he gingerly climbed on, maneuvering himself so that he was parallel to Josh, the two of them leaning back against the wall the bed was shoved against.

Evan smiled. "I should probably introduce you two because I doubt you've met considering Angel here likes to fuck and run. Angel, Leo. Leo, Angel."

Damian quashed the absurd urge to shake Josh's hand. *What did he normally do when he was introduced to a new scene partner?* He turned his head slightly to the side, enough that it seemed as if he was looking at Josh without actually looking at him. "Hey."

"Hi, Leo."

Apparently oblivious to the simmering awkwardness on the bed, Evan waved Adam closer, the cameraman picking up his camera and positioning himself. "We'll start off the usual way. Quick chat. I'll ask you both some questions. Just be natural, but remember your persona when you answer. You know how our subscribers get if you contradict yourselves. I swear they take notes and refer back to them."

Damian nodded, dimly aware of Josh next to him doing the same. *Were they actually going to do this?* Without even talking about it first.

Glancing around, Evan checked that the camera light was on before slipping into his usual patter. "Hi, Angel. Hi, Leo. It's great to see the two of you together at last. Leo, you haven't filmed with us for a while. What have you been up to? I bet our subscribers have missed you."

No one was more surprised than Damian was when intelligible words actually managed to come out of his mouth. "Oh, you know, studying. I've been busy with exams." He forced a smile, aiming it straight at the camera. "It's good to be back, though."

"I bet." Evan's gaze moved across to Josh. "We've seen you recently, Angel, but then, our subscribers would probably riot if we didn't give them their regular dose of you and that beautiful cock."

Josh's laugh didn't sound particularly forced. Was Damian the only one struggling with this? Josh found it easier than he did to think of it just as work. But surely that didn't include fucking your boyfriend on camera. What they did was private. Damian didn't want to share it with a load of subscribers sitting in their bedrooms with their hands wrapped around their cocks.

"What do you think of it, Leo?"

He dragged his attention back to Evan. "What?" Before he could respond, Damian worked out what the question had been about—Josh's cock. The very thing he'd had his lips wrapped around the previous night for a prolonged amount of time. "It's nice."

Evan's eyebrow quirked. "Nice! Wow. That's almost an insult. Or maybe a challenge. Right, Angel? Let's see if he can come up with a better adjective than nice once you're fucking him with it." Evan leaned forward, a strange gleam in his eye. "Shall I tell Angel our little secret, Leo?"

"Secret?" Damian was genuinely clueless over what he could be referring to.

"Yeah! That you've been desperate to do a scene with him ever since you first started here, all those months ago. I think that's why you've gone shy. You're good with the shy boys, though, aren't you, Angel?"

"Sure. He won't be shy for very long once I get my hands on him."

Evan winked. "Then we should stop delaying and get to the action." He gave the usual wave of his hand which signaled Adam to stop filming, waiting till the camera was off to continue. "Usual thing, guys. We'll shoot a few minutes of kissing and groping. Keep your underwear on for that. Hands can go down it, but let's build a bit of anticipation up. Then we'll start with Angel blowing Leo before we go into a sixty-nine. As for the sex positions, we'll go facedown, doggie, missionary. I'll give you the usual signal when I want you to swap to the next. That alright with you boys?"

Despite the fact that Damian felt like he was either going to spontaneously combust at any moment or pass out, he managed a jerky nod. He was sat next to his boyfriend, the guy who only had to look at him to make him hard, and he'd never felt less horny. This was going to be the worst scene ever.

On autopilot, he turned, taking his first look at Josh since he'd walked into the room. He'd been wrong to assume that Josh was fine about what was about to happen. He looked about as edgy as he'd ever seen him. Their gazes clashed, Damian's question about how they were going to get out of this reflected in his boyfriend's eyes. But Damian guessed the answer was they weren't, not unless one of them was prepared to come clean about the reasons.

He paused, waiting to see if Josh would say something. He knew Evan far better than Damian did. It would be better coming from him. When Josh stayed silent, Damian steeled himself. He could do this. *They* could do this. After all, it was nothing they hadn't done hundreds of times. The only difference was a camera and two men watching them. They just needed to pretend no one was there and forget that it would mean thousands of subscribers would be watching it later while they jerked off.

Damian carefully placed his hand on Josh's bare thigh, twisting around to bring their lips closer together. Josh leaned in at the same time but misjudged the distance, their heads bumping together. They both pulled back. Not a problem. Mistakes happened. Evan could cut that bit. Damian swung his thigh over Josh's, straddling him and trying to ignore Adam moving alongside them to get closer in order to negate the fact that Damian had turned his back to the camera. Josh's hand moved to grasp Damian's ass, but there was a weird tentativeness there that Damian wasn't used to. Damian wiggled, finding the cock underneath his ass to be completely soft. That was going to take a lot of work. Mind, his wasn't any better. *What were they supposed to be doing?* Kissing, right. He braced his hand against Josh's chest, covering his boyfriend's lips with his own. They remained resolutely closed, no matter how much he tried to tease them into opening with his tongue. It was like trying to kiss a mannequin.

Evan coughed loudly. "How long are you two going to keep this up? Because I gotta tell you guys, if I devised a list of the least sexy things I've ever seen in my life, you'd definitely feature, and possibly be right at the top of it. I'm not sure I can take any more of this excruciating awkwardness. What about you, Adam?"

Adam started to chuckle. "It's pretty bad. It's like they've both turned into virgins. Want me to keep filming just for amusement value? Or do you want me to stop?"

"You may as well stop."

Damian twisted around to look at Evan, surprised to see amusement rather than annoyance on his face. "Sorry. We're just taking a bit longer than usual to warm up."

Evan's eyebrow quirked. "Oh, I think we all know you're not going to warm up." He cocked his head to the side. "Funny though. I only usually see this sort of thing when two guys hate each other or"—he paused dramatically—"they're a couple in real life, who suddenly go camera-shy when demonstrating their private business to all and sundry."

Josh sat up so fast that Damian found himself tipped off. Luckily, it was in the direction of the empty side of the bed, rather than the floor. "You know!?"

Smirking, Evan leaned farther forward on the chair. "I know what?"

Damian leaned back against the pillows, watching the interchange between the two men.

Josh sighed. "That we're a couple. And all of this was some sort of twisted set-up to get us to admit the truth."

The director's lips curved slowly upward. He placed a palm flat over his chest, his eyes twinkling. "Josh, darling. Careful, or you might end up hurting my feelings. Even more so than they are already. You know, considering that one of my biggest stars and someone I consider a friend, and have done for years, has been keeping a huge secret from me for however long."

It was probably way past the time that Damian involved himself in the conversation, if only to support his boyfriend. "It wasn't like that. We thought you might be annoyed."

Adam coughed to get Evan's attention. "You still need me, mate... or?" He inclined his head toward the door.

Evan waved him away. "No, you go. But I want that bit you just filmed. Reckon I'll play it whenever I'm feeling down. Best comedic remedy ever." He turned his shrewd gaze to Damian as Adam exited through the door. "And I'm only annoyed because you didn't tell me. What sort of ogre do you take me for? I like my boys to be happy." He winked at Josh. "I've got to admit I'm surprised, though. You were always so anti-extra-curricular fun with everyone you've ever filmed with, no matter how much they threw themselves at you. So how long?"

Glancing over at Josh, Damian let him take the lead, just in case he wanted to tell a little white lie to soften the extent of their subterfuge. He hesitated before telling the truth. "Six months. Well, it will be next weekend."

Damian smiled at the fact that Josh knew exactly how long they'd been together. But then, he shouldn't have been surprised, really. His sexy boyfriend had turned out to be quite the romantic too. He'd even found himself whisked off to Paris one weekend. It hadn't quite replaced Blackpool in his memories as best weekend together, considering that was where all the magic had started, but it was a pretty close-run thing.

Evan arched his eyebrows so high, they almost disappeared into his hairline. "That long. Wow! You two are quite the pair of secretive squirrels."

"How did you know?" Damian was interested to know the answer to Josh's question himself.

"You were seen last weekend. Kissing and canoodling in the corner of a bar."

Josh let out a snort of laughter. "Evan, man. You're a porn director. You can't be using words like canoodling."

Evan eased himself off the chair, carrying it over to the side of the room to leave it standing against the wall. "Maybe not." He turned back around, his eyes narrowing as they alighted on both of them. "I can assume, right, that seeing as you've been together so long, neither of you are about to up and quit on me?"

Josh rolled his eyes. "Now we get to it. The real reason for you going out of your way to lure us here. I don't have any plans to at the moment." He glanced over in Damian's direction. "And Damian's been doing less scenes anyway." Josh held his hands up in the air in a gesture of surrender. "Nothing to do with me, by the way, before you start getting uppity. He's just been busy."

Evan crossed the room, coming to stand at the end of the bed. "Yeah, busy with you. So of course I blame you." He sighed. "Anyway, it is what it is. And before you ask, no, you're not getting paid for that shameful show of non-eroticism you just put on. I'll leave you to it, though, and lock the door. How's that?" He left the room with a wink.

Relaxing back against the pillows, Damian exhaled. He felt like a naughty schoolboy who'd been caught doing something he shouldn't. It didn't help that Josh had dissolved into hysterical laughter as soon as the door had closed and they were alone. Damian rolled onto his side, waiting until his boyfriend had finally calmed down. "I'm glad at least one of us thinks it's funny." He poked him in the ribs. "Also, if you'd told me you were filming today, I would have known what Evan was up to."

Josh leaned up onto his elbows. "Oh, so you think Evan didn't ring me late last night claiming that he desperately needed my help? I thought it was a bit fishy, that I was replacing someone else and then he had to find yet another replacement.

But you've got to admit that our performance was amusing." He leaned over, his lips finding Damian's easily, as if to demonstrate the difference. With no cameraman, Damian melted into it easily, their previous awkwardness a distant memory. They kissed lazily for a few minutes until Josh maneuvered Damian on top of him, their bodies fitting together perfectly. There were definitely no soft cocks in the room now. Damian clasped his hands together on Josh's chest, leaning his chin on top so that he could look at him. "It must have been when we were in the Black Bull last Saturday. I told you to keep your hands off me."

He got the incredulous look he was expecting, Josh rising to the bait immediately. "You said no such thing. I seem to remember someone having a little bit too much to drink and virtually climbing on top of me. And you wouldn't take no for an answer. We're lucky we didn't get thrown out of there, especially when you were trying to get your hands in my pants."

Damian smiled at the memory. It was no wonder they'd been outed, but then, it wasn't as if they'd set out to keep their relationship a secret from Evan. It had just happened. Both of them must have been far too wrapped up in the other to note the presence of anyone from the studio. He wondered who it was that had blabbed. Probably someone trying to score points with Evan. Either that or they'd been jealous. He took a moment to consider how he'd have felt pre-Blackpool weekend if he'd gone to a bar and seen Josh making out with someone. It would probably have lain somewhere between complete sadness and wanting to rip the other guy's face off. He leaned forward, dropping a kiss on his boyfriend's nose. "That's one of the many reasons you love me."

Josh's hands fastened on Damian's ass, pressing it more firmly against his crotch. "Your wandering hands?" He grabbed one of them, pushing it under the waistband of his underwear until Damian's palm met a rapidly thickening cock. "I'll admit that I'm quite partial to them. That and a few other things."

"Tell me more."

A glint appeared in Josh's eye. "Well, there's the fact that my family loves you. Even that new boyfriend of my sister's, who I have to say seems remarkably straight and very unlikely to grope you at family events, thinks you're great."

Damian narrowed his eyes. "Carry on." He wrapped his hand around Josh's cock giving it a gentle squeeze for incentive.

"God! You're so needy." The smile on Josh's face belied his words. "You're the best fake boyfriend who turned into a real one that I could ever have asked for. Sex with you that weekend at my parents' house was incredible and it has only gotten better since then. You're funny, you're sexy, and you never complain about me wanting to bottom the majority of the time. You're practically perfect. You know I love you. I tell you all the time."

Hard as he tried, Damian couldn't keep the goofy smile off his face. Josh did tell him all the time but it never hurt to hear it again. "I love you too." He glanced around the room, an imp of an idea coming to him. The camera was off. The door was indeed locked because he'd heard Evan lock it just as he'd said he would on the way out. He turned back to his boyfriend, his hand tightening around his cock with intent. "You're so fucking gorgeous, Angel. Have I ever told you that?"

Surprise blossomed on Josh's face, his eyebrows rising at Damian's use of the alternative name. But it didn't take him long to get with the program. He slid his hand inside Damian's underwear, his warm palm grasping his ass. "No, you haven't, Leo. I knew you had a thing for me, though. I could tell by the way you looked at me."

He arched his back, pushing his ass more firmly into Josh's hand. He let his voice drop to a husky whisper. "How did I look at you?"

A slow smile transformed Josh's face. Damian could see the porn persona slide into place. For some reason they'd never role-played this scenario. Other stuff, yes. They were both pretty adventurous in the bedroom. But when were they ever going to get the chance to play in this exact same setting again? He waited for Angel's answer, not disappointed when it came. "You couldn't take your eyes off my cock whenever you were talking to me."

Damian sat up, wriggling out of his underwear, his erect cock standing proudly. "That's because you didn't stop fondling it whenever I was in the vicinity, Angel. Teasing me with what I couldn't have."

Josh flipped him onto his back, coming down on top of him, his muscular body fitting between Josh's thighs. "Oh, you can have it, Leo. You can have all of it."

Damian smiled. He loved this man. It was amazing how a crush had turned into such a fulfilling relationship. There was no way he was letting him go any time soon. They already had plans to move in together once they'd finished their degrees. Right now, they were going to have some fun. He groaned in Josh's ear. A perfect exaggerated porn moan. "Show me, Angel. Show me what you can do with that big cock."

IF YOU ENJOYED THIS book, you might be interested in pre-ordering Cain's story. You can do this at the following link.

[mybook.to/ALittleTooEager][1]

CAIN'S BEEN SECRETLY in love with his best friend's older brother for as long as he can remember. Joining an adult film company was meant to solve his problems. Or at least the one where he struggles to get a boyfriend. But real life repeats itself. Apparently, Cain's good enough for a roll in the hay, but not good enough for a relationship. Perhaps he doesn't hide the geek beneath the muscular exterior as well as he thinks.

Lawyer, Nicholas Hackett's hiding his own secret. One that he guards closely and has no intention of revealing. Especially not to his little brother's best friend, no matter how much misplaced hero worship he might throw his way. The best thing he can do is stay away from him. Only, that's getting more and more difficult.

When a family wedding throws them together, secrets are bound to come out. And maybe both men are going to be shocked at how the other reacts.

There could be surprises all round.

---

[1] http://mybook.to/ALittleTooEager

SIGN UP TO MY NEWSLETTER to access a free 15k stand-alone story The Second Act as well as bonus chapters for my Too Far series and Edge of Living. Sign up through my website or at the following link. Download links are in the Welcome e-mail received after sign-up.

newsletter sign up[2]

---

2. http://eepurl.com/dw-7nH

Thanks, from H.L Day

THANK YOU SO MUCH FOR choosing to read this book. You've made me really happy. How could you make me even happier? Well, you could leave a review. Then, I'd be ecstatic. :)

About H.L Day

H.L DAY GREW UP IN the North of England. As a child she was an avid reader, spending lots of time at the local library or escaping into the imaginary worlds created by the books she read. Her grandmother first introduced her to the genre of romance novels, as a teenager, and all the steamy sex they entailed. Naughty Grandma!

One day, H.L Day stumbled upon the world of m/m romance. She remained content to read other people's books for a while, before deciding to give it a go herself.

Now, she's a teacher by day and a writer by night. Actually, that's not quite true—she's a teacher by day, procrastinates about writing at night and writes in the school holidays, when she's not continuing to procrastinate. After all, there's books to read, places to go, people to see, exercise at the gym to do, films to watch. So many things to do—so few hours to do it in. Every now and again, she musters enough self-discipline to actually get some words onto paper—sometimes they even make sense and are in the right order.

Finding H.L Day

WHERE AM I? I OFTEN ask myself the same question.

You can find me on Twitter[1].

You can find me on Instagram[2]

You can find me on Facebook.[3]

Send me a friend request or come and join my group -Days Den[4] for the most up to date information and for the chance at receiving ARCs

You can find me on my Website[5]

Or you can sign up to my newsletter[6] for new release updates.

---

1. https://twitter.com/HLDAY100
2. https://www.instagram.com/h.l.day101/?hl=en
3. https://www.facebook.com/profile.php?id=100010513175490
4. https://www.facebook.com/groups/2214565008830022/?ref=bookmarks
5. https://hldayauthor.co.uk/
6. https://wordpress.us18.list-manage.com/subscribe?u=e4815ef5cc09451a6bcd7aaa4&id=1875e83c44

More books from H.L Day

CHRISTMAS RICHES

Opposites might attract. But does that include age?

Christmas comes early for Aiden Malone in the form of a seductive, blue-eyed stranger down on his knees. But a shocking revelation about his new "friend" has him running for the hills and cursing his stupidity before the night is out.

Tom's not prepared to give up that easily. He may be rich where Aiden's poor. Innocent in a way that Aiden isn't. And on the wrong side of twenty. But he's old enough to know what he wants. And that's Aiden. He just needs to persuade the older man to look past his hang-ups about age and wealth.

Lust and prejudice pull Aiden in opposite directions, severely testing his willpower. As Tom's layers begin to peel away, Aiden discovers the younger man's life of privilege may not be all it seems. If Aiden gives in, they could have the sweetest Christmas that either of them has ever tasted.

But Tom's about to shatter their joy with a surprise announcement. Decisions need to be made on both sides. It's down to Aiden, though, to stay strong and decide whose happiness is more important. His? Or Tom's? Because they can't have it both ways.

It's possible their relationship won't even last as long as it takes for the snow to melt.

Buy from Amazon

A Temporary Situation (Temporary; Tristan and Dom #1)

Personal assistant Dominic is a consummate professional. Funny then, that he harbors such unprofessional feelings toward Tristan Maxwell, the CEO of the company. No, not in that way. The man may be the walking epitome of gorgeousness dressed up in a designer suit. But, Dominic's immune. Unlike most of the workforce, he can see through the pretty facade to the arrogant, self-entitled asshole below. It's lucky then, that the man's easy enough to avoid.

Disaster strikes when Dominic finds himself having to work in close proximity as Tristan's P.A. The man is infuriatingly unflappable, infuriatingly good-humored, and infuriatingly unorthodox. In short, just infuriating. A late-night rescue leading to a drunken pass only complicates matters further, especially with the discovery that Tristan is both straight and engaged.

Hatred turns to tolerance, tolerance to friendship, and friendship to mutual passion. One thing's for sure, if Tristan sets his sights on Dominic, there's no way Dominic has the necessary armor or willpower to keep a force of nature like Tristan at bay for long, no matter how unprofessional a relationship with the boss might be. He may just have to revise everything he previously thought and believed in for a chance at love.

Buy now from Amazon[1]

---

1. http://mybook.to/ATS

A Christmas Situation (Temporary; Tristan and Dom #1.5)

Love conquers all. But can it survive Christmas?

Dominic and Tristan have been together for almost a year. So everything's got to be plain sailing, right? Not quite. Not if you ask Dominic. Tristan's a bundle of energy and crazy ideas at the best of times. Add in Christmas, and it's a recipe for disaster.

That's not the only issue. There's also Tristan's mysterious absences and secret phone calls to contend with. Dominic might be insecure, but he's not crazy. His boyfriend is definitely up to something, and neither family nor friends seem interested in listening to his concerns. He won't jump to conclusions this time though. He'll talk to Tristan. Only what do you do when you can't get a straight answer out of the man you love?

When Tristan's secrets are revealed, will their first Christmas together also be their last? Or is Dominic about to discover that all his worries have been for nothing?

Only time will tell.

A story containing Christmas snark; a drunk Tristan; snow; and absolutely no mention of spiders—well alright, maybe a few mentions.

Buy from Amazon[2]

---

2. http://getbook.at/ACS

Temporary Insanity (Temporary; Paul and Indy #1)

Sleeping with the enemy never felt so good.

When Paul Davenport comes face to face with the man he caught in bed with his boyfriend years before, it's hate at first sight. Well, second sight. Indy should be apologizing, not flirting. Except the gorgeous barman is completely oblivious to their paths ever having crossed before.

Despite his feelings, Paul's powerless to resist the full-on charm offensive that follows. It's fine though. It's just sex. No emotions. No getting to know each other. Just a bout of temporary insanity that's sure to run its course once the simmering passion starts to wear off.

Only what if it's not? Indy's nothing like the man Paul expected him to be from his past actions. What if they're perfect for each other and Paul's just too stubborn to see it? Forging a relationship with him would require an emotional U-turn Paul might not be capable of making.

There's a thin line between love and hate, and Paul's about to discover just how thin it really is. He can't possibly be falling for the man that ruined his life. Can he?

Warning: This book contains hate sex—sort of, lots of banter, and a pink elephant. No, really it does. Actually, two elephants.

Please note: Although this book is in the Temporary series, it occurs during the same timeline as A Temporary Situation. Therefore, both books can be read as standalones and in any order.

Buy from Amazon[3]

---

3. http://getbook.at/TemporaryInsanity

Time for a Change

What if the last thing you want, might be the very thing you need?

Stuffy and uptight accountant Michael's life is exactly the way he likes it: ordered, routine and risk-free. He doesn't need chaos and he doesn't need anything shaking it up and causing him anxiety. The only blot on the horizon is the small matter of getting his ex-boyfriend Christian back. That's exactly the type of man Michael goes for: cultured, suave and sophisticated.

Coffee shop employee Sam is none of those things. He's a ball of energy and happiness who thinks nothing of flaunting his half-naked muscular body and devastating smile in front of Michael when he's trying to work. He knows what he wants—and that's Michael. And no matter how much Michael tries to resist him, he's not going to take no for an answer.

Sam eventually chips through Michael's barriers and straight into his bed. But Michael's already made some questionable decisions that might just come back to haunt him. He's got some difficult choices to make if he's ever going to find love. And he might just find that he's too set in his ways to make the right ones quickly enough. If Michael's not careful, the best thing that's ever happened to him might just slip right through his fingers. Because even a patient man like Sam has his limits.

Buy from Amazon[4]

---

4. http://getbook.at/TimeforaChange

Kept in the Dark

Struggling actor Dean only escorts occasionally to pay the bills. So, his first instinct on being offered a job with a strange set of conditions is to turn it down. No date. Don't switch the lights on. Don't touch him. I mean, what's that all about? What's the man trying to hide? Dean certainly doesn't expect sex with a faceless stranger to spark so much passion inside him. It's just business though, right? He can put a stop to it whenever he wants.

When Dean meets Justin—a scarred, ex-army soldier unlucky in love. Dean's given a chance at a proper relationship. He can see past the scars to the man underneath. He's everything Dean could possibly wish for in a boyfriend: kind, caring and sweet. All Dean needs to do is be honest. Easy, right? But, Justin's holding back and Dean can't work out why. But whatever it is, it's enough to give him second thoughts.

They both have secrets which could shatter their fledgling relationship. After all, secrets have a nasty habit of coming out eventually. The question is when they do, will they be able to piece their relationship back together? Or will they be left with nothing but memories of bad decisions and the promise of the love they could have had, if only they'd both been honest and fought harder.

Buy from Amazon[5]
Also available in audio

---

5. http://getbook.at/KITD

Refuge (Fight for Survival #1)

If you no longer recognise someone, how can you possibly be expected to trust them with your life?

Some might describe Blake Brannigan's life in the small Yorkshire village of Thwaite as bordering on mundane. His job in a café doesn't exactly set the world alight. But, he's got his own house, a boyfriend, and a close-knit group of good friends. For him, that's more than enough to lead a contented life.

Then in one fell swoop, everything's ripped away when he's forced to flee the village with only his boyfriend for company. He doesn't know why they're leaving. He hasn't got the faintest clue what's going on, and he's struggling to understand the actions and behaviour of a man he thought he knew. A man that it soon becomes clear knows far more about what's happening than he's letting on. A man hiding a multitude of secrets.

When the true extent of what's happening comes to light, Blake is rocked to the core. Peril lurks around every corner. The smallest decision suddenly spells the difference between life and death. If Blake's to have any chance of survival in this new and frightening world, he's going to have to unearth buried secrets, figure out whether love really can conquer all, and face emotional, physical, and mental challenges the likes of which he could never have imagined.

One thing's for sure, when life suddenly boils down to nothing more than the desperate need to find refuge, priorities change. Blake's certainly have.

Buy from Amazon[6]

---

6. http://mybook.to/Refugebk1

Taking Love's Lead

Zachary Cole's new personal shopper is stunning in more ways than one. Gone is the staid, professional Jonathan. In his place is sexy, whirlwind Edgar, whose methods and lifestyle are less than orthodox. Still reeling from the experience, Zack can't get him out of his head. He needs to see him again. Even if it does involve dragging his heavily pregnant sister and her dalmatian into his cunning plan.

Sick of being dumped yet again, dog walker Edgar's pledged to stay single and put energy into finding a career more suited to an adult instead. Zack might be extremely tempting...and just happen to pop up wherever he goes, but that doesn't mean he's going to change his mind. He's got bigger priorities in life than a website designer who's after a brief walk on the wild side. Edgar's heart has taken enough of a bruising. He's not prepared to get dumped again.

Zack wants love. Edgar only wants friendship. Can the two men find common ground amid the chaos of Edgar's life? Or is Zack going to find that no matter what he does, there's no happy ending and he'll have to walk away?

Warning: This story contains dogs. Lots of dogs. Big ones. Small ones. Naughty ones. Ones that like ducks, squirrels, and lakes and ones that like to be carried. No dogs were harmed in the writing of this book.

Buy from Amazon[7]

---

7. http://getbook.at/TheZon

Edge of Living

Sometimes, death can feel like the only escape.

It's been a year since Alex stopped living. He exists. He breathes. He pretends to be like everyone else. But, he doesn't live. Burdened by memories, he dreams of the day when he can finally be free. Until that time comes, he keeps everybody at bay. It's been easy so far. But he never factored in meeting a man like Austin.

Hard-working mechanic Austin has always gone for men as muscular as himself. So, it's a mystery why he's so bewitched by the slim, quiet man with the soulful brown eyes who works in the library. The magnetic attraction is one thing, but the protective instincts are harder to fathom. Austin's sure, though, that if he can only earn Alex's trust, then the two of them could be perfect together.

A tentative relationship begins. But Alex's secrets run deep. Far deeper than Austin could ever envisage. Time is ticking. Events are coming to a head, and love is never a magic cure. Oblivious to the extent of Alex's pain, can Austin discover the truth? Or is he destined to be left alone, only able to piece together the fragments of his boyfriend's history, once it's already too late?

Trigger warning: Please be aware that this story deals with suicidal ideation and other dark themes. If this is a subject you find uncomfortable, then this book is not recommended.

Despite this, there is a guaranteed HEA.

Buy from Amazon[8]

---

8. http://mybook.to/EdgeofLiving

A Dance too Far (Too Far #1)

Love can be dangerous!

Valentin Bychkov, rising star of contemporary Russian ballet, appears to have everything: wealth, talent, success, and a face and body to match. Not that anyone can get close. Bypass the entourage and there's still Valentin's sharp tongue and acerbic wit to deal with. He may give his body freely, but his emotions are kept tightly locked away.

Max Farley's life is a simple one. All he's interested in is work, drinking, and picking up the latest in a long line of one-night stands. The way he chooses to live may not be to everyone's taste but it suits him down to the ground. He's never met anyone who's made him want to confront the demons from his past. Until now.

A show in London brings the two together. Lust brings them closer still. But if rumors of Bratva connections turn out to be true, then dangerous men wait in the wings. One dangerous man in particular, who's used to people following his orders without question.

Difficult choices need to be made on both sides. Valentin and Max need to stop playing with fire and let each other go, or face the consequences. But letting go isn't that easy where love is concerned.

And some things are worth the risk.

Warning: This book contains a snarky ballet dancer with an aversion to clothes, a little too much wall sex and an overabundance of Russian heavies.

Buy now from Amazon[9]

Coming to audio in December 2019

---

9. http://mybook.to/ADancetooFar

A Step too Far (Too Far #2)

Two men. Three identities. An unstoppable attraction.

Desperate for his luck to change, Jake Spencer manages to land a dance contract with Dmitry Gruzdev. The job has plenty of perks, including a simmering lust between him and Dmitry's hulking brute of a bodyguard, Mikhail. Life is finally looking up. Except as the shine wears off, it becomes clear that Jake's stepped into a world of darkness and depravity where Bratva answers to no one and allies are not what they seem.

Mikhail's hiding a secret: there is no Mikhail. He's simply a front for undercover operative, Ryan Harris. A means to gain access to Dmitry. Ryan's not stupid. There's no way he's going to get distracted by a pretty face, no matter how attractive Jake might be. That would be far too dangerous for all concerned. Only it's not that simple and before Ryan knows it, the line between personal and professional begins to blur spectacularly.

Lust develops into more. Secrets start to unravel. Ryan's got an impossible choice to make: keep Jake safe or maintain his cover. But how much does Dmitry know? The hunted may be about to become the hunter, blowing both men's worlds to pieces and leaving them with nothing.

Can a relationship built on lies ever lead to love?

Warning: This book contains a seductive dancer prone to getting into trouble, a gruff man who's anything but, and a villain who just won't go away.

Buy now from Amazon[10]

Coming to Audio in January 2020

---

10. http://getbook.at/ASteptooFar